BLOODSWORN

Three Vows

Val Cates

To Sara,
the best friend and moral support an author could ask for

CONTENTS

A Note from the Author:

Those of you who have read **A Gift of Name**, *my debut, young adult/fantasy novel, are already acquainted with some of the characters in this story. This is an "alternative timeline" story, as it occurs in a setting in which Abirad never existed and Eilis was raised by her grandfather.*

A few other changes have been made to characters and details from the original setting. Additionally, Eilis and Albain have been aged up a bit for this piece due to some of the mature aspects of the content.

Enjoy this new take on two of my favorite characters from **The Stolen Heir Series**!

CHAPTER 1

"How much further?"

Eilis's voice could scarcely be heard through the raging wind and torrential rain. She pulled her fur-lined cloak tightly around her shoulders as she turned her face away from the onslaught of rain. The chill of the wind seeped into her bones and caused her to shudder as a fresh gust of air slapped at her cheeks and compelled her to raise a leather-gloved hand to shield her eyes.

Her companion shifted in the saddle of his ebony warhorse. Albain was accustomed to riding day and night through all manner of conditions, often even taking his meals and sleeping while still on his horse. Such was the life of a Clanless. He lived a solitary existence, never staying anywhere long enough to call it home.

For many of his years, he had worked as a mercenary, accepting jobs that were not for the faint of heart. He had done things that he was not proud of on behalf of truly terrible people all in the name of survival.

It was by luck and through his prowess in battle that his fortune had recently changed. Albain had caught the attention of the All-Chieftain, Seamus Oakheart of the Oak Clan, and he had been permitted to remain on their lands as the All-Chieftain's guest.

While the Oak Clan had shown him hospitality, many of them still did not trust him. He took note of the way all speech seemed to cease when he passed, and the way the whispers began in his wake. They feared him. He couldn't rightly blame them for being intimidated. He was an immense force of nature, standing equally between six and seven feet tall, and he appeared all the more impressive when fully armored. His body was a honed mass of battle-hardened muscle. When in combat, his dark brown eyes shone with a bloodlust and fury that would stall any enemy in their tracks, and his shoulder-length dark hair did little to mask the hideous scars that marred his face. His skill with a sword was unmatched, and even without a weapon, he could fell countless enemies with his brute strength alone.

Albain knew he was an outsider, and while others had homes, handcrafted from strong oak and passed down through the generations, he lived in a small tent on the outskirts of the encampment. He was content to be alone, at least until he met Eilis, the All-Chieftain's granddaughter.

Now, he was her Bloodsworn, pledging his sword and his life to the protection and service of the young woman before him.

Albain dragged a large, calloused hand over his face to dispel the water that had gathered there, but just as soon as it was swept away, he found himself sputtering under another deluge of water. "Soon. Three more days, four if the rain keeps up like this."

He could see the disappointment blanket Eilis's face. He thoughtfully rubbed his beard and reassessed his response, for her benefit. "Or more."

Immediately, her expression brightened, and Albain couldn't help but to be amused by the fact she would rather endure days of relentless rain than to finally reach their destination.

They had been travelling for nearly a sennight, and with every step they drew closer to Callor's Rest, the home of Lord Selwyn Callor, the more the young woman's demeanor dampened. She had made it quite clear she agreed to this task under the greatest of protests.

The Oak Clan inhabited the borders between Allanon and Evinster, and recently, the nomadic Talvair, a barbaric race that pillaged and plundered for sport, had begun to encroach upon the lands of the All-Chieftain. While that was concern enough, there had been reports that King Ulric McGairn of Evinster had commanded the Talvair thus for the purpose of testing Allanon's borders. His eye was set on the throne of Allanon, and the Bromus clans of the borders would serve as the proving ground for his forces.

While the Bromus did not serve any sovereign directly, they had enjoyed a comfortable truce with the rulers of Allanon for hundreds of years. The monarchy left the clans to do as they pleased, and in return, when the kingdom needed aid, the Bromus helped to bolster its ranks.

However, as it was the lands of the Bromus that were in the most imminent danger, King Ruden of Allanon had taken it upon himself to use the situation to his advantage. He would send some of his royal forces in support of the Bromus, but he wanted a binding agreement of the loyalty of the clans. To this end, he proposed that the All-Chieftain send his granddaughter and sole heir, Eilis Oakheart, to meet with the King's favorite nephew, Lord Selwyn Callor, who would serve as a potential suitor.

Eilis had railed at the request, but in the end, her loyalty to her clan and the love she bore her grandfather had convinced her of the necessity of this meeting. There had been no marriage contract made, and if meeting this Lord Selwyn would help her people, was it not her duty to do everything in her power to protect them? One day, she would be All-Chieftain, and surely there would be even more difficult sacrifices than this.

❊ ❊ ❊

After a few hours, the rain began to slow, but the cruel bite of the wind increased, and even the heavy cloak around her shoulders did little to bring Eilis any comfort from the cold. Her weariness had begun to take its toll, and soon she found her eyes growing heavy.

It seemed like only a moment that she had closed her eyes, but when she opened them again, she found herself no longer on her own horse. The numbness in her arms had dissipated, and where there had once been nothing but ice in her blood, she felt warmth. She struggled to stay awake long enough to find what had caused this rather pleasant change. She leaned back against something hard and unyielding, and she felt slight pressure to either side of her. She looked behind her, and her eyes met that of her Bloodsworn protector.

Albain glanced down at her briefly before returning his gaze to the trail ahead. "You looked as if you were going to fall from your saddle. You felt half-dead with cold. I've been trying to find us some shelter. Ground is too wet to make a decent fire. Fairly certain I spotted a cave last time I was around these parts. That was some years ago, but might still usable if I can find it. Would be a good place to rest until morning."

Eilis nodded weakly and pressed her back against his chest. In response, he wrapped his own cloak tightly around them. Eilis couldn't help but to laugh slightly as she thought of how appalled her grandfather would be if he saw this happening. While he respected Albain as a warrior, the last of the Curs was not granted a place on the Council; he was still considered a Clanless.

The Cur Clan had been the most aggressive of all the clans, and when they ran out of enemies to fight, they had turned on each other. That was the world Albain had been raised in, and fighting was all he had ever known. During early life, he had watched as his clan had warred themselves into oblivion. Minor disagreements were cause for relentless bloodshed, and in the end, Albain had become the last of the Cur Clan.

The All-Chieftain had been exceedingly vigilant when Albain had begun to spend more time with Eilis. It wasn't Albain's doing. He had taken every measure to keep to himself, but Eilis had taken notice of the way he ate alone, the way he secluded himself during feasts and ceremonies, and how he spent more time talking to his warhorse than any human. She had noticed, and she had vowed to remedy the situation. She made it a point to greet him every day. When he sat alone, she joined him. When he sparred against the other warriors, she shouted his name in support, and when he returned from battles, she mended his armor and bandaged his wounds. In return, he had taken the Bloodsworn Oath, the greatest vow a Bromus could take next to marriage, and in doing so, he promised to always put her life before all other things.

Albain abandoned the path and carefully navigated his horse and Eilis's enormous, white destrier over rocky terrain. Finally, he saw the opening of a cave and quickly tethered the horses to a sturdy tree just outside its entrance.

He helped Eilis from the saddle and led her into the cave where he promptly started a fire and urged her to draw closer and warm herself while he sought something for nourishment. They had plenty of dry rations, but a hot meal was what they needed. He wasn't a brilliant marksman; the greatsword had always been his weapon of choice. However, he could manage with a bow when a situation required it, and before long, he lumbered back to their camp with two freshly killed rabbits in his enormous hands.

Soon the smell of roasted meat permeated throughout the cave, and full bellies fostered much improved spirits for both of them. Albain unfurled his bedroll and reclined his massive frame over the thin but comfortable padding. Eilis, on the other side of the fire, did the same, and soon she was peacefully dozing.

Albain watched her through the flames. For the thousandth time, he cursed himself for gazing upon her too long. He was just about to settle in for the evening when he saw her draw her cloak tightly around her. Even with the roaring fire, her entire frame shivered terribly.

He rose to his feet, crossed to her side, and knelt next to her. At first, he thought that perhaps she was having a nightmare, but then he noticed the flush of her cheeks. He pushed up the sleeve of his tunic and gently pressed his wrist against her forehead. His eyes widened in alarm as he realized her skin was like an inferno.

He rummaged through his bags for some allowary root and set to making her a cup of tea with it. Allowary was renowned for its healing qualities and was used for everything from salves to prevent infection to tonics for upset stomachs. It was particularly useful for treating fevers.

As much as it pained him to rouse her, Albain knew the fever needed to be addressed immediately or else it could worsen.

"Eilis," he said softly. "Eilis. I need you to wake for just a bit."

At the sound of his voice, her eyes fluttered open. He offered her the cup of tea, and she groaned as she tried to rise. He helped her into a seated position and sat next to her while she sipped her tea.

When she emptied the last of the cup's contents, and he was satisfied that she could now rest easily, he moved to return to his bedroll.

Her hand lightly grasped his wrist, her touch causing him to freeze in his tracks. "Do you think... Do you think you could remain here for the night... with me? The tea helped, but I still feel so cold."

He hesitated for a moment. While he wanted nothing more than to be close to her, he knew that his heart hoped for more than she would ever be able to give him.

He wanted *her*.

He wanted her smiles and her tears.

Eilis's generally serious nature belied her sense of humor, and during his time as her Bloodsworn, he had learned what could coax a genuine laugh from her. While Albain's demeanor could be best described as dour, Eilis's smile was absolutely contagious, and even he found himself affected by her moments of levity.

He had also seen her at her most vulnerable. He had been by her side when the first graves were dug after the Talvair incursion. She had tirelessly spoken with every clansman who had lost someone dear. She had extended her sincere sympathies through a listening ear as her people recalled fond memories of those whose souls had moved on. She held their hands as they wept and tried to rationalize why the Maker had taken their loved ones. All the while, she comforted them with encouraging words and a promise to ensure the departed had not died in vain. Her people had drawn strength from her, and she from them.

Yet, in the evenings when she returned to her tent and was allowed some moments of solitude, she had been unable to fight back the tears that threatened to overwhelm her and intrude upon her invulnerable façade. Sometimes she just needed to be left to her own devices and allowed a few moments to collect herself. Other times, Albain would rest his hand upon her shoulder to remind her she was not alone. Whether space or comfort, Albain gave her whatever she needed.

His observational skills as a warrior had taken on a new form as he committed to memory a study of her quirks, like how her eyes sparkled when she was excited about something, or how irritable she became when she was hungry. Albain had also taken note of that crease in her brow that appeared as she puzzled through a problem, or the way she grew silent when she was ruminating on something or was intensely focused.

He wanted to be more than her protector. In truth, she could protect herself quite well. All Bromus women were trained in the arts of combat, and Eilis was one of their greatest female warriors. She wasn't simply his charge, someone he watched over out of a sense of duty. He had never had a friend, and he supposed their companionship could be likened to that, but he could not shake the feeling that this was something more.

She was a force of nature, and she had uprooted the entirety of his being.

Never in his life had he met anyone like her, and despite his gruff and unapproachable nature, she had managed to break through his defenses and had awoken some part of him he had not known existed.

However, she was the Heir to the All-Chieftain and would one day be leader of all the Bromus. Her mother— the All-Chieftain's only child—had been killed along with her husband, Eilis's father, during a Talvair incursion. As such, Eilis had become next in line to lead their people.

She was well-regarded among their folk and was a natural diplomat. In fact, in her youth, her grandfather had reluctantly sent her to the capital city, Vericus, for two years to receive training in the ways of the royal court and to serve as a companion to Prince Trystan, a friendship that endured to this day.

While King Ruden spared no love for the Bromus, even he was impressed by Eilis, which was likely a factor in this convoluted scheme. In the monarch's mind, Eilis was the perfect bridge between the people of Allanon and the Bromus. Due to her stay in Vericus, she lacked the typical brogue that marked Bromus speech, though the accent had a tendency to slip out when she was angry. She was intelligent, level-headed, and showed wisdom far beyond her years. By her teens, her kin had taken to calling her Eilis the Wise, and this title continued to be ascribed to her, now in her twenties.

Albain did not doubt she would be an excellent All-Chieftain, but it was also one of the reasons he was reluctant to pursue her. She had a duty to their people, responsibilities to uphold, and a reputation to protect. She was the closest thing to nobility that the Bromus could claim, and he was the last of a dead clan. He could never be considered a suitable match for her.

His mind told him to make up an excuse to maintain some semblance of distance and to put the fire and several feet between them, but as she gazed up at him with pleading eyes, dark brown pools that never ceased to capture him, he knew he could never deny her anything.

He gave a slight nod and moved his bedroll next to hers. He wrapped his cloak around them, and when she pressed her back against his chest, his heart thundered with such intensity that he was worried the sound might wake her. However, his fears were for naught as he soon noted the soft, measured breaths that indicated she had again given in to sleep.

* * *

They remained in the cave for three more nights until Albain was certain that Eilis was well enough to travel. Even though her fever had broken that first night, they continued to sleep with their bodies nestled against each other. Albain constantly told himself it was simply due to her need for warmth and comfort, but when she rested her head on his chest or snuggled into the crook of his arm, he couldn't help but think that perhaps there was more to it.

He toyed with the idea of just living out the rest of their days in the cave. Things seemed so much simpler there. He enjoyed the peaceful routine they had settled into during their travels, and he knew if it were up to Eilis, she would remain in the cave forever if it meant avoiding the trip to Callor's Rest. However, her honor forced her to assert that she was well enough to continue their journey, and so they resumed their trek.

Yet, every night when it was time to rest, they somehow found their bedrolls next to each other once again. At first, Albain had allowed her to lean against him and take whatever warmth from him she desired, but soon he began to wake with his arms wrapped around her, or he would find himself laying on his back with her head resting upon his chest. He knew his intimidating reputation would be difficult to keep up if anyone would chance upon them and see the smile he wore upon his face every morning when he woke, but it was worth it.

She was worth it.

He had never before allowed his heart the grace of happiness, but at the same time, an angry gnawing began to tear at his chest. They would soon be in Callor's Rest, and the All-Chieftain had pledged that Eilis would remain at least a fortnight, but longer if she found Lord Callor desirable and a marriage contract could be arranged.

Eilis had been told she should be honored to have piqued the interest of this Lord Callor. He was said to be exceedingly wealthy, incomparably handsome, and a very learned man who prided himself on intellectual pursuits. He was also rumored to be a half-decent swordsman, though he had never seen battle.

Albain couldn't be more opposite. His life had been mired with poverty, and there was scarcely an inch of his body that did not bear scars. Most prominent among them was the deep gouge on his face that extended from his forehead to his chin. The blow that had caused it had nearly blinded him as well. It definitely caught the attention of women, but more from horror than admiration. Yet, it never seemed to bother Eilis. In fact, she had recently taken to allowing her fingers to trace the outline of his scar before letting them rest at his chin. There had been a few moments when he had felt compelled to take a kiss, but a kiss should not be taken but given, and she had not gifted him with one. Still, his heart swelled with the idea that she might, however farfetched or misguided that hope might be.

Unbeknownst to Albain, Eilis was of the same mind, and countless times she had silently willed him to press his lips against hers and claim her for his own.

The final night of their journey found them huddled next to each other by a roaring fire. Albain wasn't accustomed to building such large fires. He had always made it a point to avoid notice as much as possible during his travels. Some nights he had even gone without a fire at all, but for her, he'd build a bonfire taller than the royal castle if it meant seeing her happy.

Eilis, noticeably occupied with some thought, was quiet that night; her anxiety was nearly palpable.

"What is it?" he asked with concern.

"We'll be there tomorrow," she said softly. "Is it wrong that I still don't want to go? I mean... I know that I *have* to, but I don't *want* to. I've no interest in meeting this Lord Selwyn Callor, and I certainly have no desire to marry him."

"Might change your mind." The words stung his lips, but it was true. While he harbored admiration for her, he would never be an acceptable match as far as the All-Chieftain and the rest of her clan were concerned.

Eilis's eyes widened in abject horror. "Never! Living in a castle as some lord's lady? I'd rather not. I still intend to be All-Chieftain one day. I don't see how I could ever accomplish that if I married his sort."

"You're stubborn. You'd find a way. Lots of people have arranged marriages, and they find ways to make them work."

"I don't want to make it work." She rested her head against his shoulder and was comforted when he pressed his cheek against the top of her head.

Her heart raced in her chest; his hammered so loudly that he thought it might explode from his body. Tentatively, she wrapped her fingers around his. Their gazes locked, and neither of them could keep their emotions at bay any longer. She gently touched his cheek, the scarred one, and inclined her lips towards his. Eagerly, he followed suit, and when he felt the soft pressure of her mouth on his own, her lips gracing his in a tender kiss, he felt as if the entire world trembled.

This.

He wasn't sure what *this* was, but he knew if he died that instant, it would be with a full heart and a content soul. He felt invigorated and renewed, as if she had sparked a fire in his chest, and he craved more moments like *this*.

The effect was absolutely dizzying, and reluctantly, he broke the kiss in an attempt to recover from the breathlessness that had stolen the air from his lungs. Her brown eyes sparkled as she gazed up at him with adoration, and again he felt a faint glimmer of hope course through him. He cupped her face in his massive hands, the coarse skin of his palms and fingertips a stark contrast to the softness of her face. In awe, he lightly rested his forehead against hers.

Suddenly, his ears picked up on the faint sound of hoofbeats and breaking twigs in the distance.

Albain quickly unsheathed his sword, and before he could tell Eilis to do the same, she had already taken hers in hand.

"If you meant to surprise us, you failed. State your business!" he called, strategically positioning himself between Eilis and the direction of the noise.

"We are the personal guard of Lord Selwyn Callor," came the reply. "We are searching for his guest, Eilis Oakheart of the Oak Clan."

"You've found her," spoke Eilis, sheathing her sword.

She turned to look at her Bloodsworn, and Albain could have been mistaken, but he was quite certain that he saw disappointment and longing in her eyes, but perhaps that was merely his own desire reflected back at him.

CHAPTER 2

Callor's Rest looked like a smaller version of Elidure Castle, the residence of King Ruden. Eilis had spent time there during her youth as a guest of the royal family and had since visited it many times while calling upon her friend, Prince Trystan, or when she accompanied her grandfather to Vericus on business matters. Callor's Rest was opulent and garish, qualities that the lord of the manor likely shared.

When Eilis had learned of this agreement between King Ruden and her grandfather, she had immediately written to Prince Trystan about the situation. Her friend responded with his condolences and said it was an ill-conceived notion. He found his cousin Selwyn to be tiresome and pretentious, though not nearly as loathsome as the lord's brother, Ser Romley Callor. The prince had also stated that he had expressed his thoughts on the matter to his father only to be rebuffed and told such a match was in the best interest of the kingdom.

Eilis trusted Trystan's counsel, and therefore expected Lord Callor to be exactly as her friend had described. This made the prospect of their meeting even more undesirable, and Eilis suffered a growing sense of dread as they made their way to the grand entrance of the castle.

Upon their arrival, Eilis and Albain were received in the great hall. Despite the fact that lords generally did not have thrones (such would be seen as impertinence towards the king), Lord Callor did not seem to entertain this thought. The enormous wooden chair was taller than Albain, and it was accented with gold filigree and set with precious jewels.

The man seated at the throne was of middling height with medium length, blonde hair that he wore tied back. His eyes were a brilliant shade of blue, and his complexion fair, as if he rarely had reason to allow the sun to touch him. He was finely dressed in a white, silk shirt, dark blue doublet, and exquisitely tailored black breeches with a silken finish. He was courteous and refined, a proper nobleman.

He beckoned for Eilis to approach, and she begrudgingly complied. "Milady." He swept her hand towards his lips and planted a chaste kiss upon her knuckles. His hands were soft, so unlike Albain's, likely because those fingers had only been lifted for the purpose of summoning others to work.

She supposed he was handsome, if one was attracted to such men. However, she could not seem to stop comparing every aspect of him to Albain, and she found him wanting in every way.

"I am Ser Romley Callor, brother to Lord Selwyn Callor," spoke the nobleman.

Eilis's confusion must have been evident on her face as the man was quick to explain the circumstances of why he was receiving her. "My brother is currently in council with his advisors, but he sends his regards and his apologies for not meeting you himself. He asked that I tell you he will be holding a feast this evening in your honor to welcome you to Callor's Rest."

"I see," returned Eilis simply.

"I am so sorry you were delayed by the weather," he apologized. "The last fortnight or so has been most unseasonably cold. You must be dreadfully weary from your travels. I've arranged rooms for you in the east wing. I think you'll find them quite comfortable. There is a wonderful hearth in the great bedroom. For your servant—"

"He's not my servant," corrected Eilis. "He's my Bloodsworn."

Ser Romley appeared confused and looked to one of his advisors for an explanation.

"A personal bodyguard," offered one of the advisors.

"Ah. I see. Well, there are a number of rooms for him to

choose from near the servants' quarters. Honestly, I had thought you would have a much larger company with you given your status among your people. I would have thought you'd have more men to guard you and several ladies to attend to you."

"I don't need more than one man. Albain has the strength of ten men, and he is unrivalled with a blade," returned Eilis.

"How quaint! Perhaps while you are here, we can put your confidence in him to the test. We have a champion of our own, you see, and his constant complaint is that none of our other men present even the slightest challenge for him," explained Ser Romley cheerily.

"Any time," came Albain's deep, rumbling voice. "And if it's all the same to you, I don't intend on being separated from my charge."

"Our men are more than capable of keeping this entire castle secure. You need not worry. I can assure her safety," promised Ser Romley

"All the same, I intend to do my duty." Albain's tone was one of finality, and even the stubborn Ser Romley could see that there would be no way around this.

"Very well. I'll see that you are accommodated in another room. I believe there is one available just across the hall from where milady will be staying."

* * *

The rest of Eilis's day was spent in the company of Ser Romley, who was as insufferable as Trystan had described. He spoke at length of the family's wealth and stature and ruefully bemoaned the unfortunate pressures that a life of such wealth and privilege compelled.

"And, of course, there are many upstart families, like the Calverts—new gold nobles—who endeavor to infringe upon our holdings."

Ser Romley paused in his discourse to expound upon his

previous statement.

"Oh. That's right. You Bromus wouldn't know of such things. Well, how best to explain?" he pondered for several moments, making it seem a monumental task, as if trying to explain how trees grow to a child. Finally, he said, "Our family can trace their lineage back to the first king of Allanon. The Calverts are only a landed family because some lucky sheepherder saved our great-grandfather from highwayman. If you ask me, I wouldn't be surprised if the Calverts were behind the whole mess. They probably had one of their kin pose as a bandit just so they could make a big show of saving the king's life. False pretenses if you ask me."

"I didn't," remarked Eilis, barely concealing her apathy towards the topic of conversation.

"Well, there is something to be said for the strength of the monarchy in Allanon, an institution that the Bromus seem to eschew on behalf of their... *independence*." He uttered the last word as if it were distasteful.

Eilis fought the urge to verbally lay waste to the imbecile before her, and instead cooly remarked, "You have spoken at length of your family's importance to Allanon, and I have heard it said that the Callors are favorites of the king."

"Rightly so."

"It's so strange..."

"What?"

"I spent several years at court, but during all that time, I never saw *you* there."

Ser Romley's cheeks flushed with embarrassment, and even Albain had to stifle a laugh at Eilis humbling this peacock.

The noble quickly collected his composure again. "Anyway, these bottom dwellers, the Calverts are trying to ingratiate themselves with our uncle by presenting their misshapen daughter as a future bride for Prince Trystan. Can you imagine? As thoroughly entertaining as it would be to see my cousin marry that hobgoblin, uncle would never stand for it. Even Princess Marina of Blackwood would be a better match."

Albain dutifully remained close by, and even though he followed a few steps behind her, Eilis was glad for his company; his presence helped her to feel more at ease.

Ser Romley showed Eilis the gardens, walked with her around the castle grounds, and took her to the stables to show off his family's prized horses. Ser Romley boasted that his brother was the greatest rider in the kingdom, and his horse was of the finest stock. Lord Callor's horse was a magnificent blood bay steed with an ebony mane and certainly looked the part of a regal mount.

Next, Ser Romley took her to the library. Every bookshelf was laden with an impressive array of rare and wonderful tomes. When Eilis showed interest and inquired more about the collection, Ser Romley replied that he knew nothing about them. Reading was his brother's passion.

"Selwyn is truly the best man I know," remarked Ser Romley genuinely. "He's kind, compassionate, intelligent… but… those are all terribly boring things," he winked at Eilis who felt as if centipedes crawled beneath her skin in response to every word Ser Romley uttered.

Despite Ser Romley's glowing recommendation of his brother, Eilis was still reluctant to meet the Lord of Callor's Rest. She glanced back at Albain. His long, dark hair covered the marred side of his face as his eyes, ever watchful, passed over the vicinity in anticipation of any danger.

Eilis could not force her thoughts to stray from the kiss they had shared. She craved the pressure of his lips on her own and the light touch of his hands—strong enough to slay but gentle enough to caress.

She secretly wished they were back in the woods, alone save for each other's company.

Unbeknown to her, the Bloodsworn wished the same.

CHAPTER 3

That evening there was an incredible feast held in celebration of Eilis's arrival. The tables were piled with food in more mass and variety than she had ever seen assembled in one place. Her thoughts drifted to her homeland. The Bromus had always had enough of everything, with more to spare, but the Talvair incursions had brought more scarcity of food and goods. Her grandfather had even spoken of the need for rationing if the tides did not turn. To see such excess presented in her honor made her feel guilty that she could not load it all into a cart and send it back to her Bromus brethren.

She glanced at the roast turkey with cranberry chutney on the plate before her, but she had no appetite for it. Though her stomach grumbled, Ser Romley's incessant blathering had given her a troublesome headache.

Seated near the head of the table, Eilis silently endured Ser Romley making idle conversation as those gathered awaited the arrival of Lord Selwyn Callor. It seemed that the lord was still attending to rather urgent matters and would be further delayed, though Eilis was assured by his brother that he would be along as soon as he could manage.

Throughout the night, Eilis listened to the conversations around her. Some of the nobles and their vassals carried on in boisterous tones, but it was the hushed gossip that Eilis aspired to hear. Her visits to court had taught her that it was the words the nobles tried to hide that were often the most worth hearing. While they smiled to each other and spoke with refined civility, it was their murmurings that held their sincerest thoughts.

"How is it that wild creatures such as Bromus come here?"

"Did you see their savage queen?"

"They don't have queens; she's the granddaughter of the All-Chieftain."

"Savages. The whole, bloody lot of them."

"Did you see what she's wearing?"

"The servants said they saw her bring armor; what kind of proper lady wears armor? Did you see the sword sheathed at her side?"

"Did you hear that Lord Callor plans on courting her? Yes, really! Apparently, King Ruden thought a marriage would finally gain him the allegiance of the Bromus."

Eilis was unbothered by such drivel. Rather, it was the comments about Albain that made her blood boil.

"Did you see her guard? Big 'un that one."

"Did you see his face? If I had a face like that I'd pray for death!"

"How do you think he got it? He looks like the devil himself spit him out."

"That's the Cur!"

"Cur? Looks like someone should put that dog out of its misery."

"Would you be the one to suggest it? He's likely to beat you to death with your own arm."

"The Cur! I've heard tales of him! They say he killed twenty men singlehandedly."

"Looks like he's right for it."

"Well, I find him interesting. You know what they say about Bromus men, don't you? They turn the bedroom into another kind of battlefield, and they don't quit the field until the job is done."

This last comment drew Eilis's attention. It came from a tall, slender woman with alabaster skin and red hair. She had introduced herself to Eilis earlier as one of Lord Callor's cousins. Eilis couldn't ignore the gnawing feeling in the pit of her stomach. She could not abandon the thoughts of her growing affection for him, and the fact he had drawn the eye of someone else made her uneasy.

Eilis glanced behind her. Albain's expression was impassive, but his eyes were alert, taking in every detail of the room and its inhabitants. Ser Romley had insisted he join them at the table for the feast, but Albain persisted in seeing to Eilis's safety from his post just behind her.

Ser Romley wasted no time in enjoying the vintage wines that had been brought from the wine cellar for the occasion. He offered a glass to Eilis, who politely declined.

"More for me," he said and quaffed the contents in a single gulp.

Eilis desperately wished she could simply retire for the evening. Much of the conversation around her did not sustain her interest as it revolved around courtly gossip.

Ser Romley noticed her lack of enthusiasm and did his best to encourage conversation. Periodically, he would lean over to whisper something to her about one of the other guests at the feast or to ramble on and on about the Callor family history.

"By rights, the crown should have been Selwyn's, but he was denied his birthright. Our father—Maker rest his soul—was first in line to the throne."

"Your father was firstborn?" asked Eilis. "I thought King Ruden was the elder brother."

Ser Romley snorted. "No, our father, Prince Henry, was set to inherit the crown... until he had a falling out with his father, King Theden. Good old grandad passed him over and gave the whole bloody kingdom to our uncle instead. We've done all right for ourselves. Vast holdings, plentiful wealth, beautiful ladies," he paused and winked at a blonde woman across the table. "But had fate been different, had things gone the way they were supposed to, then I'd be a prince right now and not some sodding knight. But it will all work out in the end. My brother intends to set these matters right." He poured himself another glass of wine. "Are you enjoying yourself?" he asked Eilis. His breath was sour with the strong odor of wine. He had drunk far more than he had eaten, and Eilis wondered how he still managed to sit upright.

Eilis forced a smile and nodded. "Yes, thank you."

"You've barely touched your food. Shall I have something else made for you?" offered the noble. "Something more to your liking? Name it. Name anything at all. We have the best kitchen staff in the kingdom. Even my uncle, the king, envies the delicacies that grace our table."

"No, thank you. I am just weary from my travels."

"I see. I see. Then I shall accompany you to your rooms."

"That's not necessary. I'll see myself—"

"I insist!" Ser Romley pushed his chair back and had to use the table to steady himself. He drunkenly swayed on his feet and offered Eilis his arm, which she reluctantly took for the sake of propriety.

A heavy hand fell upon Ser Romley's shoulder, and it was then that Eilis noticed all the other guests were standing around the table.

"I think it best if you turn in for the night, brother," came a gentle voice.

Eilis looked up to see who she presumed was Lord Selwyn Callor. He was tall, and his sun-kissed skin contrasted with that of his paler brother. He was dressed in a simple green tunic, black breeches, and high brown boots. His long, brown hair was neatly tied. He waved a hand to beckon for one of his servants and requested his brother be taken to his quarters.

He turned to Eilis, his captivating, green eyes glistening with delight. "You must be Eilis. My apologies for my tardiness. I had rather urgent matters to tend to on behalf of the king."

In the front of the room, a group of musicians began to play a waltz, and Lord Callor offered his arm to Eilis. "If I may?"

Eilis accepted the gesture, and the lord led her to the dancefloor.

"Again, I do apologize for not being a better host," spoke the lord, his tone genuine. "I had truly hoped to be the one to receive you when you arrived."

"You need not apologize, Lord Callor."

"Selwyn," he corrected. "Just Selwyn, if you please."

Albain kept his ever-watchful gaze on Eilis. He felt a painful twinge in his chest, and as he watched Lord Callor guide Eilis in the dance, he found himself wanting nothing more than to drive his sword straight through the man's gut. Violence was as much a part of him as the need to breathe. He knew what jealousy was, though he had never experienced it before.

Eilis felt as if her feet were refusing to cooperate with the deft movements that Selwyn guided her through.

"You seem ill at ease. I hope I am not making you uncomfortable in asking you to dance with me," remarked Selwyn.

"I practiced dancing with Trystan when I stayed at court, but I was never very good."

Dancing in Allanon was far different than that of the Bromus. The waltz was like an art form, beautiful and elegant; most Bromus dance was done in celebration and fueled by raw emotion. Eilis favored the latter, and she grew increasingly frustrated at her inability to remember the steps of the waltz.

"Perhaps something less formal?" Selwyn gestured to the band, and they switched to a more invigorating tune.

"And how does one dance to this?" asked Eilis. "I don't know your steps to such a song."

Selwyn smiled. "If it's the steps that are a problem, then why don't we make our own?"

Albain could see the tightness of Eilis's expression begin to relax. Soon, a genuine smile graced her face, and he wished he were the recipient of such a gift.

While Albain stood watch, he was approached by a red-haired noblewoman with pale skin and the same striking blue eyes as her cousin, Ser Romley. Albain had heard her addressed as Lady Unger, a surname that all Bromus knew. Lord Balthus Unger was well-known for his open disdain of the Bromus and often imprisoned any of their people who so much as passed through his lands.

"Well, I think I can speak for all of us when I say that we certainly feel quite safe and secure with someone like you watching over us."

"I'm not here to watch over any of you. I am here for her." He gestured with his head towards Eilis.

"She is very lucky to have someone so... *capable*... as her protector."

Albain took note of the way her eyes lingered on his physique, and while some men would gladly accept the attention of a woman of high society, he simply wished her gone.

"So, do you—"

"Do you often make it a point to interfere with a man's duty?" asked Albain crossly.

"Ah... I see you take your task very seriously. Perhaps another time then?"

Albain merely rolled his eyes and maintained his focus on Eilis. She was now laughing at some remark Lord Callor had made, and while he loved the sound of her mirth, he was not overly fond of the cause of it.

✳ ✳ ✳

After a few more dances, Albain followed Lord Callor and Eilis as they made their way up the stairs and toward Eilis's apartments. Once there, the lord bid her goodnight and placed a chaste kiss upon her hand. Eilis gave a polite curtsy, as her grandfather had instructed her to do, and bid Lord Callor goodnight before disappearing into her quarters. Lord Callor lingered in the doorway long after she had closed the door. He seemed to be struggling with whether he should depart or knock on her door and beg her for more of her company.

Albain frowned; he knew the look in Lord Callor's eyes. The fool was already smitten with Eilis. How could he not be? The thought put Albain in a foul temperament, and he silently wished Lord Callor would be on his way already. Finally, Lord Callor turned from the doorway and gave a wordless nod to Albain before departing in the direction of his rooms.

Albain had resolved to stand guard in the hallway for the entirety of the evening as it was their first night in the castle. As promised, Ser Romley had arranged for a room for Albain directly across from where Eilis was staying, but the warrior still doubted the security of the place. As Bloodsworn, it was his duty to always see to the safety of his charge, regardless of their surroundings, and he knew that while royals put on grand facades, a place such as this was akin to a pit of vipers.

* * *

It was a few hours later when Ser Romley, eyes still bleary from drink, passed through the hallway.

"You know... between you and me... Albert, is it?" slurred Ser Romley.

Albain did not bother to correct him. In fact, the less he was forced to interact with this moron the better.

"Well, Albert, I was skeptical about this whole situation at first, but I'm quite happy for my brother. Lady Eilis is far comelier than I had expected. Though, she still looks more animal than woman in that fur cloak. I've a feeling that if she was granted some proper attire, she'd give the ladies of the court reason to be envious."

Albain fought the urge to grip the man by the throat and slam him repeatedly against the wall until he was little more than a pile of blood and bones. His fists clenched at his sides, and it took every ounce of self-control he had to not act on the violence that raged in his mind.

"And the weapon! What kind of woman brings a weapon to a feast! Still, this could work, you know? She has a certain... *fire* to her... a fire I wouldn't mind using to warm myself." Ser Romley waggled his eyebrows suggestively, eliciting a flash of rage in Albain's eyes. The young noble quickly recognized his error. "I meant no offense to your lady of course! Lady Eilis seems quite kind and honorable. Some men have a weakness for wine. Some a weakness for women. Mine is both."

"Be careful to bite your tongue in the future when you speak of her. I protect not just her person but her honor, and noble or not..." He leaned forward menacingly. "I'd kill you if it means keeping my oath."

"Again, my apologies! Sincerely! I only meant this marriage business... that's not for me. My brother is accepting of the monotony of monogamy. I know I'll be forced to marry someday, but even then, I could never be true to one woman. There are a lot of pretty women in this castle. I receive many guests. Might even have a few bastards born by foreign princesses." Ser Romley laughed loudly and clapped Albain on his shoulder.

Again, Albain was forced to muster every bit of self-control he had to refrain from striking the man down.

"You understand, I'm sure. Fellow like you must be beating back those barbarian women with a stick. I'm sure you're quite the catch among your people," persisted Ser Romley. "You must bed women left and right."

"No," replied Albain firmly.

"You're not *married,* are you? That would be bloody awful, I'm sure."

"Marriage must be different among you nobles than with our people," said Albain, trying his hardest to keep his tone even. "For us, the Marriage Vow is sacred. Once a man is married, he takes no other woman. Ever. Even if his wife passes before him."

"And that is why the Bromus are considered savages. Outdated values and a dying culture. I pity the lot of you. Good night, Albert." Ser Romley sympathetically patted him on the shoulder before stumbling down the hallway and out of view.

Albain's entire body was alight with fury, and he reminded himself why he was here. He was here to protect her, and if he acted upon his ire and gave that arrogant fool what he truly deserved, then he would likely have to fight his way out of the castle, which would put Eilis in grave danger.

Albain muttered a string of profanities under his breath. They were curses so strong that they would make even his old mercenary associates blush.

The Bloodsworn wasn't sure if he believed in the Maker. He remembered his mother had prayed every day, but as a child his attention was commanded more by his toys and frolicking outside than the scriptures pertaining to the Maker.

Since that long-expired period of innocence, he had experienced such pain and seen such misfortune in his life that he questioned the reality of such a being. Still, he hoped that if the Maker existed, Ser Romley would meet an untimely end at the edge of a blade, and that Albain would be the one holding it.

CHAPTER 4

The following morning, the Lord of Callor's Rest dispensed with the typical custom of sending for his guest; rather, he came to call upon Eilis himself. Her Bloodsworn was still dutifully standing watch outside her room.

"Good morning, Albain," Selwyn greeted.

"Lord Callor," came the terse reply.

"Did you sleep well?"

"No."

"I apologize if your quarters are not to your liking. I can have them—"

"I did not sleep."

"Oh! I see. Well, then, I commend you for your tireless protection of Lady Eilis."

The noble's compliment was met with stony silence and an impassive expression from Albain.

"Has Lady Eilis risen?"

"Aye, she has." Albain's gaze settled upon the bouquet of flowers clutched in the lord's hands.

"I... uh... they were blooming in the garden. They looked beautiful in the early morning sun. I thought Lady Eilis might like them."

Eilis, hearing voices outside her room, opened the door. "Good morning, Selwyn."

Albain arched an eyebrow in response to her informal greeting to the lord.

"Good morning, Lady Eilis."

"If I am to call you just Selwyn, would it not be fair for you to just call me Eilis? Besides, I am no lady. I am heir to the All-Chieftain."

Selwyn laughed good-naturedly. "That is fair, on both points." He offered her the bouquet. "Here. I thought you might like them. They're Maker's Breath. They were my mother's favorite flower, and fall was her favorite time of year."

"It's my favorite time of year as well," replied Eilis.

"The leaves changing and the autumn blooms are truly something to behold here. The whole garden is teeming with flowers, especially these."

"Thank you." Eilis gratefully accepted the flowers and retreated back into the room to place them in water.

The lord attempted to follow, but Albain blocked his path.

"Oh! Of course! I did not mean to seem impertinent," Selwyn apologized.

Albain merely grunted in reply.

Eilis appeared in the doorway again. "Thank you again for the flowers."

"I was wondering if you might like to see the library? It's one of my favorite places in the whole castle."

"Seen it," replied Albain curtly.

"What Albain means is that your brother gave us a tour of the grounds yesterday. However, he did not seem too inclined to tarry in the library."

Selwyn chuckled. "No, I suppose he wouldn't be. Romley inherited my father's love for hunting and sport. I believe my love of literature is my mother's good influence."

"You speak so fondly of her. You must have loved her deeply. How old were you when she passed?" asked Eilis.

"Too young," he replied sadly. "At least I still had my father to guide me, at least for a time. He passed while Romley was still in his teens, and unfortunately, I could do very little to diminish his wildness. A well-meaning older brother is no fair substitute for a father."

Eilis was reminded of the loss of her own parents at a young age. "I, too, lost my parents when I was young. Not a day goes by that I don't think about them."

"If I may ask, how did they pass?"

"An attack by the Talvair."

Selwyn was silent for a moment. "That is… truly awful. I am terribly sorry for your loss."

"And I for yours," returned Eilis. "I would love to see more of the library, Selwyn."

The lord's expression brightened. He offered Eilis his arm, and she accepted. He led her through the winding corridors and towards the massive library. As they entered, Eilis took note of the raven—the symbol of the Callor family—prominently featured in the center of the library. It had been meticulously carved from a single piece of marble and looked so lifelike that Eilis thought it might take off in flight from where it perched.

"Your father was the king's brother. He was an Elidure. How is it your family came to take the Callor name?"

"Ah, well, my mother was a Callor. She was an only child. When my father was passed over in favor of my uncle, he abandoned the Elidure name and took that of his betrothed. The Callors were an old line but their estate was modest. It was Callor's Rest—a wedding gift from my uncle to my parents—that became the new family seat. Can you believe my father almost refused it? He was a stubborn man. He never recovered from being slighted by Grandfather Theden."

"It seems your brother harbors that grudge as well."

"There's a philosopher, Martot Levette, who says there is a natural order to the world, and when it is in upset, it seeks to right itself. Yes, my uncle became king, but his rule has been defined by misfortune: the death of his wife in childbirth, revolts by peasants, the insubordination of the Harcourts. Perhaps it is a divine punishment. King Theden cast out his eldest son, and now his younger son must suffer the consequences."

"Are you truly so superstitious?"

"No, not really. Still, I can't outright deny the existence of fate. After all… you're here."

Eilis could practically feel Albain's gaze boring a hole

through Selwyn.

"My father would have been a different sort of king than my uncle. He had grand plans for Allanon, plans that would have had the other countries looking to us as a beacon of progress. He believed that part of the natural order is that all things are meant to evolve, and Allanon hasn't evolved in centuries." Selwyn guided Eilis to a particular section of the library.

"You have a truly expansive collection," remarked Eilis, impressed.

"Indeed! My mother had a voracious appetite for the written word. She curated most of this library herself. My favorite selections are here." He gestured to a column of shelves. "Poetry."

Albain frowned with disgust.

"You like poetry?" The excitement was clearly present in Eilis's tone. Reading poetry was one of her joys as well. She had even read some aloud to Albain on their journey to Callor's Rest, but he had made clear his lack of enjoyment in it.

"I do. Poetry. History. Drama. Anything but mathematics."

Much to Albain's horror, they spent the rest of the day in the library. Bored beyond measure, the Bloodsworn leaned against a wall with his arms crossed over his chest while Selwyn and Eilis alternated between reading poetry aloud to each other and discoursing on all manner of scholarly topics.

＊ ＊ ＊

Over the next few days, Eilis spent a great deal of time with Selwyn. He was charming, well-mannered, and intelligent. Like Eilis, he loved reading and even fancied himself a bit of a writer. He kept a journal and dabbled in poetry, but he also enjoyed practicing his swordsmanship and working with his hands. She was surprised to learn that he enjoyed woodworking and blacksmithing, and despite her earlier reservations that he would be a boring, stuffy man, he was a delightful conversationalist with an excellent sense of humor.

They had quite a bit in common. They enjoyed archery and horseback riding, and their personalities were such that it was easy to find topics to discuss at length. He seemed to be a wonderful man, and even his staff spoke highly of his kindness and generosity.

It did not take long for Eilis to realize he was quite taken with her.

One afternoon, as they walked in the garden, Selwyn said "Eilis, you are unlike any woman I've ever met before. Despite the strangeness of the circumstances of our meeting, I am glad to know you."

"I must be honest. When my Granda first told me of his discussion with King Ruden, I truly did not want to come here."

"I hope your view has softened on Callor's Rest... and its lord."

"It has. This has... well, it hasn't been as awful as I thought it would be."

Selwyn smiled, an expression that reached all the way to the corners of his green eyes. "That's the finest compliment I've ever received."

"I doubt that."

The lord laughed pleasantly. "From you, any word of kindness is one I value."

"You're not what I expected," admitted Eilis.

"Well, I am glad to defy your expectations. No matter the outcome of this arrangement, you will always be welcome at Callor's Rest, and my life is better for having met you."

However, as much as Eilis attempted to be polite and attentive towards Selwyn, it was Albain who occupied much of her mind.

She saw the way he stiffened when Selwyn offered her his arm or kissed her hand. She took notice of the way her Bloodsworn glowered at the lord when he placed his hand on her shoulder, or his gaze lingered too long for Albain's liking. She was cognizant of all these things, and it pained her, because she would much rather it be his affections instead of those of Lord Callor.

Selwyn was frequently called away to meet with his advisors, and it was these times that Eilis treasured most as it gave her the opportunity to be alone with Albain. They still had not discussed the kiss they had shared before Callor's Rest, and Eilis feared that Albain's feelings had changed towards her. He was quieter and more withdrawn, and when she spoke to him, his answers were terse.

That evening, alone in her quarters, Eilis sat curled in the window seat. Her knees were drawn up to her chest and her attention was devoted to the book of poetry she had borrowed from Selwyn's private collection. These were books so dear that he did not even keep them in the library. Instead, they had a place of honor on a bookshelf in his own chambers.

This wasn't the first night she had trouble sleeping. The castle was far too quiet for her liking. In the Bromus homelands, their houses were well-made but had thin walls, and people were always up and about at all hours of the day for early morning hunts or late-night discussions.

Eilis had just finished reading a particularly lovely poem about the nature of the soul when she was distracted by the sound of metal clattering upon stone. A glance out the window showed several servants bending down to collect a pile of weapons off the ground. The bottom must have fallen out of the large, wooden box they had been carrying as splinters of wood and the remnants of the box littered the ground. Hurriedly, the servants scooped up the rest of the swords and axes from the ground and carried them to one of four large carts parked in front of the main door of the manor.

Eilis spent the next hour or so watching as all manner of kegs and boxes were carried to the carts. She wondered over the contents of these vessels. She surmised that many of them, like the one that had broken, were filled with weapons. She also saw noted an ample amount of armor, both chainmail and leather, had been loaded into the carts.

She watched as the wagons left the estate and took the road that led towards the east.

CHAPTER 5

The next morning, Eilis desired to venture into town, and despite Selwyn's insistence that she bring some of his own guards with her, she brought only her Bloodsworn. The main gate out of Callor's Rest was a flurry of motion as servants ran back and forth in their hurry to load carts full of supplies, weapons, and armor.

When they reached the town, Eilis ventured from stall to stall but only lingered at the bookseller's and a small stand that sold roasted chestnuts. She bought a sleeve of chestnuts and offered them to Albain who eyed her wordlessly.

"I know you like them," she stated as she handed the piping hot delicacy to him.

They found a quiet spot under a shady copse of trees and sat in silence for several moments.

"What troubles you?" she asked him quietly.

"Nothing..." he replied stubbornly before letting out a heavy sigh. "And everything..."

"How have I wronged you?"

"You haven't. I wronged myself. I allowed myself to believe that...Well, it doesn't matter." He shook his head morosely, and his brow creased with frustration.

Eilis had never seen him so flustered. "Albain, speak plainly to me. You know I value your words."

"Why? I lack Lord Callor's silver tongue."

Eilis raised an eyebrow questioningly.

Albain averted his gaze and stared down at his boots. He wasn't accustomed to explaining his thoughts or feelings to anyone, chiefly because no one before Eilis had ever really seemed to value any insight he could provide beyond that which related to combat.

"I see how you look at Lord Callor. He would be a fine match for you." The words soured on his tongue even as he spoke them, and an immense knot formed in the pit of his stomach, leaving him feeling as if he had been punched. It pained him to say these things, but it was the truth. An alliance with the Callors, and thereby the throne, could greatly aid the Bromus against the looming threat of the Talvair.

Eilis smiled slightly. "This? This is why you've been so forlorn?"

"This amuses you?" asked Albain bitterly.

"No." She reached her hand up and gently stroked his cheek before pressing her forehead against the scarred side of his face.

Albain felt a chill run up his spine at her touch, but this moment of peace was tinged with anguish. "You fancy him, don't you?" inquired Albain, his voice serious.

"I don't trust him."

Albain's eyes narrowed. "Why?"

"Because of Ser Romley. Do you remember the night of the feast? How he kept leaning closer to me to whisper things?"

Albain nodded. "Aye. What of it?"

"He was telling me about their father, the late Lord Henry Callor. He was originally known as Prince Henry Elidure. He had been the eldest son of King Theden, and thereby, the older brother of King Ruden. As you know, it is typically the first, male heir that inherits the throne. King Theden thought Henry was unfit to rule and passed him over in favor of his younger brother, King Ruden. Henry was quite incensed by this and left court. However, when Ruden became king, he named his brother Lord of Callor's Rest, giving him the largest holdings in all of Allanon, save for those claimed by the crown."

"Interesting." Albain thoughtfully rubbed his beard. "So, you're saying had things turned out differently, Lord Selwyn Callor would have been King of Allanon."

"Exactly. I know he was drunk, but Ser Romley said something that put me ill at ease. He said, 'By rights, the crown should have been Selwyn's, but he was denied his birthright.' He also said 'my brother intends to set these matters right.' This is dangerous talk; one could even argue that it borders on treason."

"I know your nature, Eilis. You have a theory."

"Yes. What if Evinster isn't behind the incursions of the Talvair? What if it is the doing of some discontented nobles?"

"That's a serious allegation, and Lord Callor is the favorite of the king."

"Which is why I need proof before I can act. Here's what I do know. Last night, a very large shipment of supplies, as befitting an army, was sent east, and this morning, as we left, another shipment was being prepared."

"East? Towards home."

"Towards the borders, yes. And as you know, the Talvair stalk the borders between Evinster and Allanon. What if Selwyn is arming the Talvair in order to attack the borders? Perhaps he has even made some kind of alliance with Evinster."

"Why didn't you come to me last night?"

"Tell you I suspect our host, of treason? While we are in *his* castle?" she asked incredulously.

"You've a fair point."

"During my time in Vericus, I learned a few very important lessons. Chief among them is this: an ambitious noble is a dangerous one. Families like the Callors will hold out one hand in peace while clutching a dagger in the other. If they truly are planning to challenge King Ruden's claim, even Selwyn's affection for me would be secondary to such a goal."

Albain frowned.

"Albain... You need not worry about Selwyn. My mind has not changed about him. I still don't intend to marry him or any other lord. However, I will do what I must to ensure that I get the information we need so that if my theory is correct, King Ruden can be warned. Unfortunately, that may mean playing the part of the lovestruck maiden."

Albain nodded in understanding. "I don't like it, but I understand." He crossed his arms over his chest and regarded her in silence for several moments. His mind spun with the memory of their kiss, but he still did not know the true extent of her regard for him. "Anyway, you owe me no explanations, Eilis. I've been pouting like a petulant child. I've no right to. I've no claim to you."

The smallest of smiles affected the corners of her lips. "You've more claim than you know."

"Is that so?" He studied her expression, as if trying to assure himself she was genuine, though in his heart he did not doubt her. "I've got something for you. Picked it up in the town while you were getting those chestnuts." Albain rose to his feet and crossed to his warhorse. He dug around in the saddlebag for a moment before pulling out a small parcel wrapped in brown paper. He seated himself beside her and offered the object to her.

"What is it?"

"Open it."

She unwrapped it and found a small, red, leather-bound book of poetry. Her eyes lit up with delight. "Albain, you hate poetry!"

"Aye. It pained me to purchase it knowing I was supporting such drivel..." he said with a wry smirk, "but... I know you fancy it."

"Thank you! I love it!" She reached up, wrapping her arms around his neck, and he pulled her into a tentative embrace that deepened the longer he held onto her.

She quickly glanced around the area, and satisfied they were not being watched, she pressed her lips against his, and again, the giant of a man became undone in the wake of her tenderness. His hand rested on the small of her back, and without warning, he pulled her into his lap, causing her to emit a giggle of delight.

He knew better than to hope for her heart. Years of pain had taught him that hope is a dangerous thing. Still, in the back of his mind and the depths of his soul, he could think of nothing else.

* * *

When they arrived back at the castle, Eilis was directed to the training yards, where Selwyn was overseeing the combat exercises of his personal guard. As soon as Eilis reached the yards, the lord caught sight of her and eagerly beckoned for her to join him on the dais from which he was observing.

Selwyn gestured for Eilis to sit next to him while Albain dutifully took up his position just behind her.

The lord reached for Eilis's hand and pressed it to his lips. "Eilis, you look lovely today, as usual."

"Thank you, Selwyn."

"My brother is performing quite well, wouldn't you say?" He gestured to Ser Romley who was engaged in a sparring match with one of the guards.

Albain snorted. "If you call that bit of prancing and dodging sparring."

Selwyn appeared amused by his comment. "I suppose by *your* standards it would seem as such. They call you The Cur, do they not?"

"Aye."

"I've heard tell of your rather fearsome reputation. They say the devil himself would think twice before engaging in combat with you. I've heard it said there are few who could best you in battle."

Albain's lips curled into an intimidating grin. "No. There is *no* man who can best me in combat. A few have come close, like the bastard who gave me this," he gestured to the ghastly scar on his face.

"If I may be so bold as to ask, how did you come by that scar?" inquired Lord Callor curiously.

Albain spit upon the ground but offered no further explanation, answering the lord with only an uncomfortable silence.

Ser Romley, having finished his match and overhearing their conversation, flipped the visor back from his helmet and exposed his smiling face. "I bet I could come close."

Albain snorted in derision. "You could try. You'd fail. *Miserably*. But you could try."

"That may not be a wise idea, Ser Romley," spoke Eilis with concern. "My Bloodsworn does not speak out of arrogance or exaggeration of his abilities."

"We'll see," came Ser Romley's reply.

Albain knew Ser Romley wouldn't prove to be much of a challenge, but the prospect of any kind of combat excited his senses. The moment he stepped into the sparring area, every nerve in his body was exhilarated into action.

The news that The Cur would be sparring with Ser Romley spread like wildfire, and Eilis and Selwyn were soon joined by a large group of people eager to see the match. Everyone from kitchen staff to the nobility present at Lord Callor's court flocked to the training yard.

Among them was Selwyn's cousin, Lady Gismene, the same woman who during the feast had spoken so suggestively about Bromus men. Lady Gismene's gaze was firmly fixed on Albain as she whispered to her ladies in waiting. This was something that did not escape Eilis's notice, and she suddenly understood how Albain must have felt when seeing her with Selwyn.

Ser Romley took his time in preparing, but Albain was eager for a fight.

"Get on with it!" called Albain. "You think you'd have this much time to tighten your armor in the midst of battle?"

Ser Romley grinned in reply. "I would if my enemies had to get through soldiers like you first."

Albain spat at the ground. "I'm no soldier. Bromus don't have soldiers. We have warriors."

Ser Romley finally finished his preparations and moved closer to Albain. He spent several moments dancing around the veteran warrior, which caused Albain to become impatient with the noble's cautiousness. Eventually, Ser Romley moved within striking range, and it was then that Albain began to rain down an impressive flurry of blows that sent the noble scurrying away from him.

Albain struck with impressive strength and precision, making short work of Ser Romley, and it was merely minutes into the match when the knight fearfully conceded to the superior warrior.

Ser Romley had to be helped from the sparring area by two of the guards, and Albain could not suppress his look of satisfaction upon seeing the pompous twit so quickly dispatched.

"Father would be so proud," teased Selwyn. He's turning in his grave to see you beaten so easily."

"As if you could do any better!" retorted Ser Romley, nursing a nasty cut above his eye.

Selwyn considered this for a moment. "Far better than you."

"Prove it!" challenged Ser Romley.

Albain stabbed his greatsword into the ground before him. "Lord or not, I don't intend to go easy on you. If he hadn't yielded when he did," he gestured to Ser Romley. "He'd be much worse for wear."

Selwyn rose to his feet and directed his servants to bring him his armor and weapons. "I wouldn't ask you to. Maybe I'll surprise you."

Murmurs of excitement erupted within the gathered crowd as the onlookers eagerly discussed the spectacle they were about to behold.

"Hmph. Not likely," replied Albain dismissively.

He glanced to Eilis who looked equal parts concerned and pleased. He knew how much Eilis enjoyed watching him fight. Like a true Bromus woman, she was impressed with strength and skill in battle. Of course, she also enjoyed flowery words and pretty dancing. He felt inept with the former and avoided the latter at all costs, but for her, he'd prance about like a foolish prat if it meant bringing her joy.

Selwyn finished donning his armor. Holding his shield in one hand and his helmet in the other, he crossed to Eilis and gave a slight bow. "Eilis, if it is not too forward, might I beseech from you a kiss... for luck? I may very well need it!" he said with a good-natured laugh.

A few of the men chuckled in response and the women tittered and gossiped over the lord's request. Such an outward show of affection from the lord was certainly a surprise, especially to one such as a Bromus.

Albain froze, his gaze fixed on Eilis. He saw through the guise of delighted shock as she met his eyes, and in them, he saw reluctance and apology. He remembered what she had said before, about doing her duty for her people. While he hoped with all his might she would somehow refuse Lord Callor's request, he knew she must agree to it for the sake of appearances, and it sickened him.

The sight of the lord's lips pressed against Eilis's was enough to set Albain's blood boiling. He remembered the tenderness of the kiss that he and Eilis had shared mere hours before, and to see the lord now taking something he so treasured incensed him. Albain, malice in mind, took great delight in the opportunity to exact his rage on this foolish lord.

A cry of delight went up from the crowd followed by the sounds of laughter and applause in encouragement of the lord's show of affection. In hopes of masking the obvious ire that was present in his eyes, Albain tore his gaze away and directed his attention towards readying his weapon.

Selwyn, his sword in his hand and his shield at the ready, stood across from Albain. Albain had watched Lord Callor spar before, and as was his custom, the warrior had already taken stock of the man's many weaknesses in battle. Selwyn was slow to raise his shield, and his footwork was sloppy. His blows, while decent enough, would be no match for someone as strong as Albain. When it came to speed, Selwyn had the advantage. While Albain was quick enough, his true abilities were his strength and precision.

Albain did not allot Lord Callor the same time to prepare, and as soon as the lord dropped into position, the Bloodsworn attacked with a relentless assault, forcing the noble backwards. Selwyn struggled to deflect the blows with his shield, but a well-placed strike from Albain knocked the shield from his hand, leaving him struggling to parry with his sword.

Albain took advantage of this by slamming his boot into the lord's chest, which sent him tumbling upon the ground. Without hesitation, Albain brought his sword down upon the noble, connecting his blade firmly with Selwyn's chestplate and causing the man to cry out in pain from the force of the blow. The lord quickly scrambled to his feet, but Albain was too much for him. The seasoned warrior brought his sword down again and again, rendering Lord Callor's off-hand useless before spinning around behind him and slamming his blade into the noble's back.

Cries of encouragement for Lord Callor came from the crowds, and Selwyn seemed to draw strength from this. He began to use his speed offensively and managed to land a blow or two against Albain's armor. The warrior glanced towards the stands to see Eilis's eyes fixed firmly on him and him alone, and he drew his own strength from her gaze. He drove his elbow into Selwyn's breastplate before using his blade to sweep his legs out from under him. Lord Callor scrambled to his feet again, and Albain smashed his gauntlet into the man's helm, knocking it clean off his head. He brought his fist across in a brutal punch that connected firmly with the noble's face, instantly darkening his eye and sending a gush of blood spurting from his nose.

Despite the abuse, the lord persisted in trying to continue the fight, but another crushing blow from Albain left the noble on his back in the middle of the training yard. Albain brought his sword down again and there was a sickening crunch as his blade connected against Selwyn's arm, causing him to cry out in pain.

"I yield! I yield!" cried Lord Callor.

Albain, filled with bloodlust, moved forward to strike again. He raised his sword above his head, but Eilis cried out his name. "Albain!"

He was snapped out of his battle fury by the sound of her voice, and a thrill rushed through him when he saw the look of admiration upon her face. Feeling generous, Albain extended a hand to help Selwyn to his feet.

"Well done, Albain," said Eilis, with pride in her voice.

Albain gave a slight bow to his lady.

"Lord Callor, I hope you are not too injured from this contest. I had tried to warn you of my Bloodsworn's might," spoke Eilis.

Selwyn laughed weakly. "I should have heeded your warnings. It was a fair match." Despite his words, as he glanced over to Albain there was a peculiar expression upon his face, as if he was searching for something.

CHAPTER 6

Eilis was seated in the great hall with Ser Romley while Selwyn was having his wounds tended. It was just the two of them as she had called for a bath to be drawn for Albain. Despite the Bloodsworn's insistence that he remain by her side, Eilis wanted to grant him a few well-deserved moments of respite, and he had begrudgingly agreed to her request.

"Your guard... er... Bloodworn, was it?" began Ser Romley.

Eilis nodded.

"He leaves quite an impression. I now see what you meant on the day you arrived. With a guard like him, you'd need no others."

Eilis was pleased by this acknowledgment of Albain's abilities. "Yes, he is arguably the most skilled of our warriors."

"Is it true that Bromus women are taught to wield a blade?" he inquired with curiosity.

Eilis smiled slightly. "Yes. From the time we are young."

"Intriguing... A strange sort you Bromus are." He gingerly leaned back in his chair, his body still aching from his match with Albain. "Well, your Bloodsworn managed to catch the attention of many of the nobles. They'll probably all be begging him to train their guards. And that's not the only sort of attention he's captured." He grinned suggestively, and Eilis felt her stomach sink as she realized what he was insinuating. "Our cousin, Gismene, has a bit of a... ah... reputation... when it comes to building *relations* with foreign dignitaries... and their protectors. Her husband is a crass old fool twice her age and three times as wide, so she finds diversions elsewhere."

* * *

Albain made his way to his quarters, and moments later, servants appeared to draw him a bath. Once they had departed, he quickly undressed and sank down into the steaming tub. Despite the soothing warmth that the water provided to his tense muscles, he quickly washed as he was eager to return to Eilis's side. He hated to leave her alone for even a moment, but he certainly didn't care to smell like the wrong end of a pig either. He dried himself, wrapped a towel around his waist, and pulled a fresh set of clothes from his travel bag. Albain never bothered to unpack, even for extended stays; experience had taught him one always had to be ready to depart at a moment's notice should relations quickly sour.

There was a knock at the door.

"What do you want?" he demanded crossly.

There was no reply, but the knocking continued and became more insistent.

Albain sighed in irritation and whipped open the door. He had expected to see a servant summoning him to dinner; however, he was instead met with the sight of Lady Gismene Unger. Since the feast, he had overheard a great deal of talk about her. Many of the guards had openly bragged about how they had bedded her, and she had quite a reputation for being very *appreciative* in chambers.

"What do you want?" repeated Albain gruffly.

"That's hardly a greeting for a lady of nobility, especially one who has taken the time to congratulate you on your match with Lord Callor."

Albain grunted. "Congratulations? For what? It was far too easy to best him. Come and see me when I've had an actual challenge."

"Well, I certainly wouldn't refuse seeing you again under any circumstances." Her gaze lingered on his bare chest and broad, muscular shoulders.

He moved to close the door, but the woman quickly pushed into the room.

"I need to return to my duties, so you need to—" he began.

She ignored the chairs in the room and crossed directly to his bed, upon which she seated herself. "I'm sure Lady Eilis will be just fine for a while longer. Let us take a few moments to get to know one another. After all, I am sure we will be seeing quite a lot of each other in the days to come."

Albain crossed his arms over his chest and frowned at her in annoyance. "What are you on about?"

"It's no secret that my cousin intends on proposing to Lady Eilis. He is most taken with her, and the king is sure to support his request."

Albain's breath stuck in his throat. He, of course, knew it had always been a possibility, but he had pushed it as far from his mind as possible.

"Your lady will of course say yes; she'd be a fool not to. Then, perhaps, when she has all the guards of Callor's Rest to see to her protection, you can be spared for another lady in need." She smiled up at him expectantly.

Albain glowered down at her. "You misunderstand. A Bloodsworn's vow is for life. I am hers and hers alone."

Lady Gismene's slender fingers trailed to the laces at the front of her bodice. She tugged ever so slightly on them in an attempt to entice him. "I'm sure Lady Eilis would give you leave to serve elsewhere if needed."

During his mercenary days, Albain had once been sent a whore by an employer who wanted to give him a "bonus" after a successful job. However, Albain had no interest in bedding wanton women and making bastards, so he had sent her away without a second thought. He knew when he was being propositioned, but he had never been approached by a woman so willing, much less a noblewoman.

Albain couldn't help but laugh. "That's where you're wrong. I think it's time for you to leave."

"Am I not as worthy of your protection as her? She is merely the kin of a Bromus chieftain. I am a woman of noble blood. Not to mention, I have certain qualities she lacks. For one, I don't look as if I stumbled out of the woods, and secondly, I don't need blades to protect me. Plenty of men would lay down their lives for a chance to secure my favor."

"Then let *them* do it," shot Albain. "My duty is to Eilis, and it will always be to her. My blade and my body have been sworn to her protection, and I'd never leave her service... for any reason or anyone."

A strange spark of recognition passed across Lady Gismene's face, and suddenly it appeared as if some truth was dawning on her. "You speak of her more as a lover would than a guardian. Tell me..." She rose to her feet, and her hand came to rest on his immense bicep. "*How* do you serve her? Perhaps you'd like to show me."

Albain could bear it no longer. Wordlessly, he scooped her up into his arms. She gave a cry of delight as he neared the bed, but he bypassed this entirely and made his way to the door. He swept the door open and dumped her unceremoniously in the hallway just as Eilis rounded the corner and came into view.

Eilis, a startled expression upon her face, glanced down at Lady Gismene, who was frozen in shock on the floor, then up at Albain, who was still clad in only a towel. Her gaze locked on his muscular form, and he couldn't help but smirk as her face reddened and she averted her eyes.

Lady Gismene, in a fit of rage, cursed under her breath, dusted herself off, and stomped down the hall. This left Albain and Eilis alone in the corridor. For several moments, she just stared at him, her mouth slightly agape. She looked as if she wanted to say something but thought better of it. She shook her head as if to dispel some strange effect that had overtaken her, then moved to the door of her chambers just across from Albain's room.

Albain grinned wolfishly in response to her speechlessness. Feeling emboldened, he said "What's the matter, *my lady*? Does this please you?" he teased.

Eilis glanced back at his bare torso, then at his smiling face. Again, she seemed to be plagued by a loss of words. Finally, she managed to choke out "Come and... see me... immediately." A look of horror passed over her as she realized the implication of her words, and her cheeks reddened with embarrassment. "I...uh... I mean... after you've put some clothes on!"

❊ ❊ ❊

Albain dressed himself in an olive-green roughspun tunic and brown trousers. He pulled on a pair of old, leather boots that had seen better days and snatched up a studded leather jerkin to wear until he had a moment to properly tend to his soot black armor. He found himself missing his Cur Clan tartan kilt and the quickness a lack of armor brought him. The Bromus did not typically wear armor when they were on their own lands unless there was a threat of attack.

He knocked softly on Eilis's door, and upon hearing no reply, he called out her name. When she did not respond again, he tested the handle, and finding the door unlocked, entered.

"Eilis?"

She was asleep on her side, her hand resting on a small, red book. With satisfaction, Albain noticed it was the book of poetry he had gifted to her. He contemplated allowing her to rest, but a glance out the window revealed it was getting dark, and he didn't want her to miss her evening meal. He summoned a servant and told him to relate that Lady Eilis was quite exhausted and would be taking her meal in her rooms. He figured no one would protest as Lord Callor would not be attending supper since he was still licking his wounds from the thrashing that Albain had given him.

After the food arrived, Albain sat next to Eilis on her bed and gently shook her shoulder to awaken her. Her eyes flitted open, and when she saw Albain, a genuine smile spread across her face.

"Am I dreaming?" she asked softly.

Albain shook his head. "Do you often dream of ugly brutes with hideous scars?"

"No. But I do dream of you."

Now it was Albain who was rendered speechless. He tenderly pressed his hand to the side of her face and stroked her cheek with his thumb. He fought the urge to kiss her; he knew such an action would not be without risk as they could be interrupted at any time by Lord Callor or one of his servants.

Albain rose from the bed and spread the food out on the small table in the center of the room. He pulled a chair out for Eilis before beckoning for her to join him.

"You seemed tired. I thought we might dine together tonight." He spoke as he pushed her chair in for her.

"This is starting to seem like a proper courtship, Albain." Her cheeks quickly reddened. "I didn't mean to... to imply that we are..."

Albain gave a rare chuckle of amusement, and his laughter was like music to her ears. "Imply that we are *what* exactly?"

"I... I suppose I'm not sure. May I speak plainly?"

"*Always* speak your mind to me. I wouldn't have it any other way."

"I know what *I* want, but... what of your intentions, Albain... for *me*?" She bit her lip, a gesture that he had learned she often did when she was nervous.

"What troubles you?"

"When I was speaking with Ser Romley, he implied Lady Gismene had taken an interest in you."

"She has," confirmed Albain.

"And what of you for her? She is... beautiful and highborn."

"Beauty fades... and a pretty face can't conceal a rotten soul," he said meaningfully. "And you know I don't give a shite when it comes to station. Besides, you saw us in the hallway."

"I saw you stark naked save for a towel and her just outside your room," responded Eilis, averting her eyes.

Albain regarded her quietly for a moment then laughed.

"Ah...Jealousy, is it?" he said teasingly.

Eilis reddened, revealing the truth of his assertion. "Perhaps."

He considered this for a moment. "Eilis, I'm not about to go cavorting with some harlot while you are under my protection. After all, it is my duty to keep you safe."

"Yes... Of course." There was a note of disappointment in her voice, and Albain knew she hadn't understood his meaning.

"Though... It's not the only reason I refused her." He leaned back in his chair and admired her beauty. "She paled in comparison to you."

Eilis brightened considerably.

"I was in a towel because I had just gotten out of the bath when she came pounding on my door and pushed her way in. When she tried to make herself comfortable, I showed her out by dropping her in the hallway."

"You... you what?" Eilis laughed and shook her head in disbelief.

"I want no part of that woman, or any other, except..."

His mind told him he shouldn't, that it wasn't safe to do such things here of all places, but his heart wasn't about to waste any time listening to such logic.

Albain leaned across the table and pressed a tender kiss upon Eilis's forehead, before marking a path on her cheeks, and finally coming to rest on her lips.

"Happy? You have me sounding like one of those bloody awful poets you like so much."

In reply, Eilis pushed her chair back from the table and took his hand in hers. The feel of her palm against his sent a warm sensation through his entire body, and he felt his face flush even more as she led him towards the bed.

She reclined against the pillows and gestured for him to join her, a request that he was more than happy to oblige. He longed for the nights when they had slept side by side, and he was thrilled by the prospect of being close to her again.

Instinctively, he did all he could to ensure they would not

be seen in a compromising position. He crossed to the door and turned the lock. He debated pushing a chair or the table against it for added security and to slow down anyone who would try to enter, but he knew that would be awfully suspect. Furthermore, he assured himself that unless someone thought Eilis was in danger, they would at least have the decency to knock and announce themselves before entering. He closed the heavy drapes to prevent anyone from seeing into the room and crossed to the bed where Eilis awaited him.

He kicked off his boots and lay down next to her. She closed the distance between them and Albain was greeted with another kiss. His mouth moved against hers, tentatively at first then more passionately.

She matched his enthusiasm with her own. Her fingers curled into his hair and came to rest upon the nape of his neck. A slight hum escaped her lips as if willing him to continue.

His lips marked a path down the front of her throat and along the side of her neck before ceasing just above her collarbone. He raised his eyes to hers, as if asking her approval to continue, and his unspoken question was met with another passionate kiss.

He continued in his attention to her, his lips leading him down the bare skin at the top of her blouse. When he reached the fastening, he hesitated out of respect for her, and she reached to the thin lace of leather and unbound it, allowing him to continue his exploration. Her body gave a slight shiver as he gently trailed kisses down one breast, then the other. Suddenly, she sat up and simply removed the garment entirely, leaving her bare from the waist up, save for her silver, oak tree necklace, a family heirloom and a symbol of her status as the All-Chieftain's heir. It dangled just above her ample breasts, and Albain's gaze was drawn to it like a moth to the flame.

He sucked in his breath in admiration of the beauty before him. He rested on his knees, and Eilis moved to hers as she wrapped her arms around the taut muscles of his back and kissed him hard on the mouth as if to bring him back to reality.

He put his hands on her waist and pulled her against him,

and she responded by relieving him of his jerkin and discarding it upon the floor. The feel of her mouth upon his neck and her hands as they danced across the sharp lines of his back sent shivers down his spine, and soon her fingertips had found their way into his tunic and set to exploring the well-defined muscles of his abdomen.

She lifted the bottom of his tunic and helped him to remove it before it joined the growing pile of clothes on the floor. Another kiss further ignited the passion between them, and when they parted, they were both nearly breathless with need for one another.

He left it to her to set the pace, her hands and lips exploring every inch of his neck, torso, and back. No further clothing was removed, and despite the constant throbbing feeling from places below, he was content to lay next to her, the bare skin of her back pressed against his chest as he cradled her in his arms.

"I don't want you to go," she said quietly. "I miss sleeping next to you."

"As do I." He knew they would soon have to reclaim their clothes from the floor, and that he would have to depart for his own room, but he wanted to savor this moment. He pulled her tightly against him and smiled as he heard a sigh of contentment escape her lips.

This.

CHAPTER 7

The next morning, Eilis visited with Selwyn and inquired after his well-being. His face was swollen, and his nose was heavily bruised. His eye was a deep shade of purple, and there was a jagged gash on his forehead. He was noticeably limping, but the worst of his injuries was his arm, which had been broken during the combat. It had been placed in a sling to immobilize it, and he had been given an elixir of allowary root and other healing herbs to abate his pain. Despite his condition, he was in good spirits, and he bid Eilis to accompany him as he held court for the day.

Unfortunately, it was quickly revealed that Lady Gismene had been correct regarding her cousin's intentions.

All the nobles in the castle and surrounding area had been summoned to Callor's Rest. At first, Lord Callor held court for the grievances of the local townsfolk. This mostly consisted of tax matters and domestic disputes. Then, he spoke with a few of the other nobles on mundane matters such as trading deals and inquired about the cost of laborers for a new project he was working on. Then, quite suddenly, he asked Eilis to come stand next to him near his throne in the great hall.

Taking one of her hands in his, he turned to face her, his green eyes alight with excitement, and his voice filled with anxious anticipation. "Eilis, when I first set my gaze upon you, my initial thought was that you looked like one of the warrior queens of old, brilliant, strong women who served as the heroines of the stories my mother told me when I was a child. My second thought was of your beauty, and now, as I have been given the opportunity to know you better, I am struck by your wit, your kindness, and your grace."

Eilis felt a sinking feeling in her stomach. Despite the kindness of his words and the genuine affection in his tone, she did not like where this was going.

"As you know," continued Selwyn, "it was the desire of my uncle, King Ruden, that you come here so that we may meet, and discuss the possibility of a marriage contract. He spoke with great regard for you, and I know my cousin, Prince Trystan, holds you in the highest esteem. It is with his royal highness's blessing, here before my friends and family, and in honor of the continued friendship between the Bromus and the people of Allanon, that I humbly ask for your hand in marriage."

Eilis was frozen in shock. They had only been in attendance at Callor's Rest for less than a fortnight. In fact, she had been looking forward to the prospect of returning home should she be able to acquire the proof they needed to confirm Lord Callor as a traitor or prove his innocence.

As much as she tried to remain focused on Lord Selwyn, her gaze drifted around the room. The expressions on the faces of the other nobles could only be described as surprise, and upon a few of them, disgust. This did not bother her in the slightest. Rather, it was the look of horror on Albain's face that gripped her heart. They locked eyes for the briefest of moments. They had both known this could happen, but neither of them had been fully prepared for it. He quickly averted his eyes, his gaze practically boring a hole in the floor.

He knew that she had to. Didn't he? If for no other reason, then to buy them more time to further research what was truly happening in this place.

Eilis chose her words very carefully. "Lord Callor, you are, indeed, the most wonderful man and most gracious host that I have ever had the occasion to meet. Nothing would bring me more pleasure than to be your wife. However..."

The look of elation on the lord's face quickly dispelled. "Then you refuse me?"

"No, no! It is not in my power to give my full consent. I accept your proposal, but unfortunately, I cannot act on it without the blessing of my grandfather."

Albain smiled slightly. Brilliant woman. She was buying more time.

"Yes, of course! I'll send for him at once!" Eagerly, Selwyn took Eilis's hand in his own before turning to the crowd. "I know that some of you may have reservations regarding this union, but I must assure you, that not only do I act on this out of the nature of my heart, but out of my love for my people. An alliance with the Bromus will help to solidify our strength as a nation, so that we may continue to stand against the threat of Evinster. I ask that you treat my betrothed with the same respect that you give me, and may you all be warned that if any of you should bring offense to her, you do so at your own peril."

It was a thinly veiled threat, and an effective one. Certainly, there would be dissent to this union, but the lord had made his position clear; he would not tolerate any disrespect to the woman who stood next to him. For a moment, Eilis almost admired him for it. In truth, Selwyn had many traits that would commend him to be an excellent ruler and a wonderful husband, but despite the admiration he had for her, she could not return it.

The lord continued. "To celebrate our impending nuptials, I would like to hold a grand celebration with all manner of festivities and a tournament. This is to be held in six weeks as it should give sufficient time for the marriage contract to be agreed upon by both my uncle and the All-Chieftain."

He turned back to Eilis, and cupping her cheek in his hand, proceeded to formalize the agreement with a single, but prolonged, kiss.

While the crowd cheered in support, Eilis could practically feel the waves of tension radiating from Albain.

Despite Lord Callor's desire to spend time with his new bride-to-be, he needed to write to her grandfather and his uncle, have his advisors draw up the marriage contract, and tend to planning the celebration to honor her. Telling her it would certainly take well into evening to accomplish all his tasks, he gave her a parting kiss and asked if she'd meet him in his chambers for breakfast the following morning.

❊ ❊ ❊

That afternoon, Eilis decided to take the opportunity to travel into town again so she could be alone with her thoughts... and Albain. They passed most of their time in the bookstore as Eilis was on the hunt for another book on herbalism.

While she had lived at King Ruden's court, she had studied under Prince Trystan's personal tutor, an exceedingly wise man named Fenustus. He had been delighted when Eilis had shown an aptitude for herbalism, something his princely student sorely lacked. Even after her departure from Vericus, Fenustus had continued to send her large volumes and his own written observations on the discipline. She had always been eager to read anything he sent her, and she had learned a great deal about identifying plants; creating salves, tonics, and powders; discerning poisons; and treating ailments and injuries.

Normally, Albain would have lamented having to spend most of the afternoon at the bookstore, but instead, it served as the perfect opportunity to claim another kiss from Eilis. The entirety of the store was filled with long rows of bookshelves that went from floor to ceiling. It was practically a maze, and it was easy enough to obscure themselves from the shopkeeper's view, especially as there were no other patrons present at the time.

Albain's hand rested on the small of her back, and she stood upon her tiptoes to entreat his lips to meet hers. He lifted her body slightly, a gesture that forced her to suppress a giggle, then carefully supported her against one of the bookshelves as he lovingly wove a trail of kisses down the side of her neck before returning to her lips again.

"You're mad, you know. We should be more careful," she whispered to him.

"That old codger is half-blind, and you know very well there's no one else in here but us. However, I can stop if you'd like."

Her eyes widened in disbelief. "Don't you *dare* stop."

"As the lady commands." He let out a soft sigh as she traced the line of his jaw with her mouth. "I don't think I'll ever complain about having to follow you into a bookstore again."

"As much as it pains me to say, I think it best that we return to the castle."

Albain gave an exaggerated groan. "Very well."

They exited the bookstore and made their way to the weathered town stable where their horses were tethered. As they approached, Albain heard Eilis's horse whinny and watched as his own reared on his hind legs. He and Eilis exchanged a quick glance before sprinting towards the stable.

"No! No! Get back!" a high-pitched voice wailed.

Albain reached the stable first. A boy, his shaggy blonde hair falling over his terrified eyes, was crouched in the corner. He was a wisp of a lad and likely no older than nine. Albain's horse had positioned itself in front of Eilis's destrier. The large, black beast snapped its teeth at the boy which caused a sharp shriek to escape from the kid's lungs.

Albain seized his horse's reins and spoke soothingly to it. "There now, boy. Calm yourself." He ran his hand against its muzzle. "There now."

Eilis crouched next to the child. "Are you all right?"

The boy whimpered but gave a slight nod in reply.

Albain glowered down at him. "Awfully foolish to risk your life for a handful of silver coins."

"What?" asked Eilis.

The Bloodsworn gestured to the worn, leather coin purse clutched in the boy's hand. "He took it from our saddlebags. That's why your horse whinnied. Then this brute," Albain rested his hand on his horse's nose, "cornered him. You're a poor thief, boy. Perhaps you had better reconsider your chosen path."

Eilis helped the child to his feet.

"I'm not a thief," stated the boy, his blue eyes fierce with indignation.

"Then what would you call someone who steals from

others."

The boy sighed and rolled his eyes. "Fine. That's fair. But the coins aren't for me."

Albain arched an eyebrow questioningly.

"There was an accident with the plow, and the horses got spooked and broke loose. My Da got hurt. He don't get around so good now. My Mum has been trying to manage the farm, but we lost my big sister Emily last winter. Da says the fields are a mess and the crops are no good."

"So that's why you took the silver," observed Eilis, her tone sympathetic.

The boy nodded. "I do my best to help, since I'm the man of the house while Da is laid up. It's been awful hard, and my baby sister is always hungry."

"I'm so sorry to hear that," spoke Eilis. "What's your name?"

"Sebastian. Same as my Da. But my Mum calls me Lark on account of the fact I like to sing so much. She teaches me lots of songs, and I sing them to Lydi when she fusses."

"Well, Lark, how do you think your mother would feel to know you were doing such things?" asked Eilis gently.

"I don't think she'd like it very much. Y-You're not going to tell her, are you?"

"Depends. Are you going to keep trying to rob strangers and risk getting yourself killed?" demanded Albain gruffly.

"No. I promise I won't. I'll find some other way to help."

Albain snatched the boy off the ground and plunked him down on the saddle of his warhorse.

"L-look. I'm very sorry." Lark held the coin purse out to Albain.

"Keep it," he responded flatly. He swung into the saddle behind the boy.

The boy nodded and placed the coin purse back in the saddle bag for safekeeping. "Where are we—"

"Market."

"The market? But why—"

The boy's questions were met with a stern expression from

59

the Bloodsworn. Lark's mouth snapped shut and he inquired no further about their destination.

Albain gave Eilis a meaningful look. It was as if something passed between them; she suddenly understood his intentions.

Albain knew what it was like to struggle. He knew what it was like to feel desperate, to be driven by the hunger in one's belly. In Lark, he saw the image of his younger self reflected back at him.

Eilis mounted her horse and followed after Albain.

When they reached the market, Albain and Eilis each took a burlap bag and began stuffing it with all manner of food and goods.

The boy, still unsure of what was transpiring, followed after them in a daze.

Albain took a doll off from a shelf and placed it at the top of his burgeoning bag.

"Is there anything else you think your family would like?" asked Eilis.

The boy bit his lip in thought. "Strawberries. They're Mum's favorite."

Eilis added two cartons to her bag.

"I think you'd like my Mum. She's the kindest woman in the whole world, and she takes real good care of me and Lydi."

"She sounds lovely."

"And my Da, he's a good man. He works really hard to try and give us everything we need. He's real smart, too. He knows everything! And he tells fun stories. At night, when he tucks me and Lydi in, he tells us tales of sorcerers and magic. You know, like from the olden times."

"I like stories, too. That's why Albain and I were in town today. We were at the bookstore."

"Albain. The big fellow? Is he your guard?"

"He's my Bloodsworn."

"What's a Bloodsworn?"

Eilis hesitated. Of course, she could define Albain's station in its most literal terms, but to do so seemed to diminish all he was to her. "Albain has many roles. He's my protector, sworn by blood to give his life for mine. He is bonded to me."

"Oh! Does everyone have a Bloodsworn?"

Eilis shook her head. "No, but I am very lucky to have him." Her gaze drifted to her beloved.

"I haven't seen you around here often. Are you from far away?"

"We're Bromus. My Granda is the All-Chieftain."

"The All-Chieftain! He was in one of Da's stories! The Old Oakheart! Seamus the Strong they call him!"

"That's him."

"Wow," breathed the kid. "I thought maybe Da was making him up! He said the Old Oakheart killed two Talvair with his bare hands!"

"Partly right... it was three," replied Eilis with a wink.

Once both sacks were full, Albain plucked the boy off the ground and placed him back in the saddle.

Lark directed them back to his family's farm. It was a shriveled piece of earth, and Albain guessed that this wasn't the first year the family had endured lean living and hardship. As they approached, a woman carrying a toddler on her hip, emerged from the house. She was followed by a tall, lanky, ebony-haired man who leaned heavily on a hastily constructed wooden crutch.

"Lark? Are you all right?" asked the woman.

"All right, Mum!" called the boy as Albain helped him off the horse. He promptly bounded towards his parents and gave them a lingering hug.

"He hasn't caused any trouble, has he?" The injured man, presumably the elder Sebastian, ruffled his son's hair. His tone was light, but his green eyes reflected worry.

Albain shook his head. "Not a bit."

"It was kind of you to bring him home," spoke his mother. "It was getting on in the day, and I was starting to worry. I had sent him into town for a handful of potatoes hours ago."

"We got those!" exclaimed the boy brightly. "And lots more! My new friends got all this for us!" he explained. "The lady is Eilis. She's really nice. The big man is Albain. I think he tries to make people think he's grouchy all the time, but he's really nice, too."

Albain's face reddened which was met with a snicker from Eilis.

Albain and Eilis set the sacks down on the porch, and Lark proudly presented the contents. His parents' eyes widened with surprise.

"All this... for us?" There was awe in Sebastian's voice. "I don't... I don't know what to say."

"I think we can start with thank you." Lark's mother clutched Eilis's hand in her own. "I don't know what we did to deserve such good fortune, but you... I don't think you realize how much you've helped us. This is truly a blessing from the Maker."

Lark held the doll out to his little sister. "Here, Lydi. This is for you."

The child let out a squeal of delight and clutched the doll to her chest.

Albain tossed Lark the coin purse from the saddlebag. "Mum! Da! Here!" He held the coin purse out to his parents. It was heavier now as Albain had slipped a few gold coins into it before giving it to him.

The boy's parents were rendered speechless.

"We best be going," announced Albain. "You've a good lad."

"And he's lucky to have you both," added Eilis. "And this little one." Eilis touched Lydi's cheek causing the girl to giggle.

Lark sprang forward and dashed towards Albain. "Will I see you both again?"

"Perhaps."

"Just in case I don't." Lark wrapped his arms around Albain's legs in a firm embrace. "Thank you, Albie! Thank you, Eilis! For everything!"

The Bromus heir and her Bloodsworn mounted their horses and pointed them in the direction of Callor's Rest.

"Albie," Eilis said aloud. "I rather like it."

Albain rolled his eyes, but Eilis saw the smile that tugged at the corners of his lips.

CHAPTER 8

Eilis woke with the sun. She quickly dressed and was eager to have a few moments to enjoy Albain's company before making her way to breakfast with Selwyn. However, when she opened the door, Selwyn was patiently seated in the hallway across from her room.

"I told him you'd be along once you woke, but he insisted on waiting for you," spoke Albain flatly from his usual post just outside Eilis's door.

"What brings you so early, Selwyn?"

Selwyn struggled to his feet, and Eilis offered an arm to steady him. "A gift. I had it commissioned for you from our finest, local seamstress." He held out a parcel to her and eagerly watched as Eilis opened it.

Inside was a beautiful blue shawl, meticulously detailed with gold thread. The craftsmanship was truly exquisite. Most impressive was the silver oak tree, so pristine in its design that it looked as if its leaves might sway with a passing breeze. In its branches rested a raven.

"In honor of our union," explained Selwyn. "I had thought that once we are wed, we might include your own heritage in our heraldry. The ravens of Callor's Rest will find respite in the branches of the mighty oak."

"It's magnificent, Selwyn." Eilis felt a pang of guilt. While her instincts told her that there was more to Lord Callor than met the eye, she knew his affections for her were true. She reminded herself that despite his grand gestures, the man before her was likely responsible for arming and supporting the Talvair, the ferocious ravagers who had killed so many of her people.

"Here. Allow me." With his good arm, Selwyn delicately draped the shawl around Eilis's shoulders and stepped back to admire her. "You look absolutely radiant."

"Thank you, Selwyn."

"Shall we go to my chambers for breakfast? I had the chefs prepare sweet pumpkin pasties and fresh apple cider."

Eilis accompanied the lord with Albain, not attempting to mask his scowling, following close behind.

When they arrived at Selwyn's apartments, Albain took up his post outside the main door. He would have much rather been within the room, but while Lord Callor afforded him far more freedom than his own guards, he had requested some privacy for himself and his betrothed. Still, if any foul play occurred, there was no door in all of Allanon that would have kept Lord Callor safe from Albain's wrath.

The pumpkin pasties were divine, and Eilis made a mental note to put one aside for Albain.

"I wanted to take a moment to thank you," spoke Selwyn.

"Thank me?"

He nodded. "Yes. You have brought great joy to my life in such a short time. I must admit, the life of a lord is more solitary than one would think. Yes, there are always people around, but they are often here out of service or, in the case of my cousin or other nobles, their own selfish ambitions."

"You mention ambitions. What are yours? To be a poet? A scholar?"

Selwyn chuckled. "I wish that were so. No... the world is changing, and if the nobility doesn't change with it, the monarchy as a whole will suffer."

"How so?"

"You've met my uncle. He is very set in his ways. Which were his father's ways... and his father before him... and on and on. You understand my point."

"I believe I'm following."

"Being a noble used to mean something. Now, people like my brother squander wealth and influence. They would rather gossip about each other than bring about any significant change in the world."

"And what changes would you make?"

"I would see Allanon restored to its former glory. Blackwood. Evinster. Grey Hall. They consider Allanon a lesser power. Our influence has faded in the world. We used to be looked to as a prime example of what a country should be. Now... we are a relic."

"Have you spoken to your uncle about your thoughts?"

"I have... with the same result one could expect from talking to a stone wall. Unfortunately, if change is to occur, it will have to be after his time."

"Prince Trystan is quite progressive."

"With all due respect, as I know you and my cousin have an enduring friendship, he is too much his father's son... too complacent."

"I don't see that at all. Perhaps you do not know your cousin as well as you may think."

"Perhaps. However, that is enough talk of such matters. I would rather speak of matters of the heart. As I was saying earlier, this life... it can be a rather lonely existence. You have brought new light to my life. I enjoy your company immensely, and I am honored that you accepted my proposal."

"I am honored that you asked."

"So, have you finished the last book you borrowed?"

"I have."

"And your thoughts?"

"Varegeux's words speak to me. I enjoyed his views on the dual nature of the human soul."

"Ah. The Beast and the Divine. 'Within every man exists two halves, locked in eternal battle over the soul. The Beast is the primal urge and pride of man...'"

"'While the Divine is his temperance and humility,'" finished Eilis.

"Yes! Very good!"

"Do you have any others by him?"

"Of course. Come." Selwyn reached out his hand, which Eilis took, and led her to the bookshelf that housed his private collection.

Her eyes scanned over the books he had collected. She was familiar with many of them. In fact, one of the poetry books was the same title that Albain had gifted to her. There were plays, collections of wisdom by famous philosophers, histories, but there was one tome in particular that attracted Eilis's attention.

Selwyn placed another book by Varegeux in her hands. "There you are, my love. This is his second piece. I hope you enjoy it."

✳ ✳ ✳

It was several days later when a messenger arrived from Vericus. In his hand, he bore two letters: one for Lord Callor from King Ruden, and the other to Eilis from Prince Trystan. As Eilis broke the seal, she was greeted by only the briefest of messages. In her friend's messy scrawl was simply written,

Eilis,

HAVE YOU GONE MAD?

Trystan

Eilis wanted nothing more than to tell her oldest and dearest friend of her suspicions regarding Lord Callor, but while she trusted him entirely, she was reluctant to reveal any information to him as she feared the message could be intercepted. She determined that if she was able to secure the proof she needed, she would tell Trystan when he arrived for the celebration.

She finished donning her armor, fastened the sheathe for her sword to her belt, and made her way into the hallway where

Albain was waiting.

The castle was exceedingly empty as Selwyn and his brother had departed that morning to visit their cousin, Lady Gismene, at her estate. Half the castle staff and the best of the trained soldiers had gone with them, so they would have the training yard to themselves.

Eilis had always favored fighting with an axe and shield, as was the style most prevalent among the Oak Clan, but Albain had encouraged her to broaden her knowledge of combat and had been training her to better use a sword.

Wordlessly, they made their way to the training yards and entered the sparring ring. Albain wasn't wearing his usual armor and instead had decided upon chainmail and a pair of padded leather pants as they allowed him to move more quickly and have better range of motion. He had even opted for a lighter broadsword over his coveted greatsword.

Eilis dropped into her swordfighting stance, and Albain gestured for her to close with him. She swung her blade to his left, but he easily parried it. She attempted to land another blow, but Albain was exceedingly quick for a man his size, even more so when he wasn't encumbered by his plate armor. Finally, she was able to find an opening in his defenses and managed to strike him on his sword arm.

"Well-struck, Eilis. Let's see how you do when you're on the defense." Albain switched to a more aggressive style, which left Eilis to parry a flurry of hard and fast blows.

"Albain?" Her voice was barely audible over the sounds of combat.

"Aye?" Despite the interruption, he did not cease his assault.

"I love you."

Albain felt as if she had taken a warhammer to his chest, and his shock and hesitation had resulted in allowing her a distinct advantage in combat. She used the opportunity to sweep his legs out from under him, and the warrior fell hard on his back while his opponent held the point of her sword just over his heart.

Had it been real combat, she would have landed a killing blow.

While he was stunned by his own folly, he was absolutely stricken by her words.

Still laying upon the ground, he propped himself up on his elbows. "That was a dirty trick," he muttered. "I can't believe I fell for it."

"It was no trick," replied Eilis, sheathing her sword.

"You picked a fine time to say it. As if I'm not already at your mercy."

"Do you think it's any easier for me, having you always within my reach, yet somehow always out of my grasp?"

He studied her face, as if searching to confirm the truth of her words. "I'd caution you against saying such things unless you truly mean them. If you grant me your love, I can't promise to let you change your mind and watch you go off and marry some royal fool." His tone was joking, but his eyes conveyed his seriousness.

"I wouldn't have said it unless I meant it."

"Then say it again."

"I love you."

Suddenly, he enacted a lesson he had attempted to teach her time and time again: Your opponent is never fully defeated until he is dead.

In a swift motion, he swept her feet out from under her, causing her to topple forwards only to be caught in his arms.

"And I love you, Eilis… Always."

CHAPTER 9

It was nearly a sennight later when they were able to find time to themselves again. Albain, with a basket in his hand, appeared at Eilis's door. "Do you think we might be able to slip away for a while? I want to show you something."

She glanced down at the basket he held. "And what do you have in mind?"

"I told you. I want to show you something. It's a bit of a ride, but worth it. I discovered it on our journey here. I came upon it while I was out hunting. I meant to take you there, but I never got the chance as we encountered Lord Callor's men."

"You had my consent at *slip away*. If I remain in this place any longer, I'm bound to go mad. Selwyn is meeting with his council all day today. I'll send him a message that I'm going out riding. That will satisfy him well enough."

They saddled their horses and rode along at a leisurely pace. When they reached their destination, Eilis was greeted by a beautifully picturesque waterfall hidden in a secluded part of the forest. Albain tethered their horses to a tree and spread out a large blanket on the forest floor. He stretched out on his back, and Eilis curled up next to him, laying her head upon his chest, much like she had done upon their travels to Callor's Rest. They remained like that for a time, enjoying the silence and time away from the hustle and noise of the castle as well as the serenity that their stolen moments together always brought to both of them.

She cupped his cheek with her hand and carefully examined the long, deep scar that marred his face. Its origin was a mystery even among the Bromus, and therefore, a source of speculation. Most agreed that it had been suffered in battle while others argued he had run afoul of dangerous characters in his youth.

"It was my father," he said quietly, answering her unspoken question.

She paused in her attentions to look into his eyes and saw the pain that resided there.

"My father was the greatest warrior the Cur Clan had ever known, but he was a hard man. My mother died when I was young... died on the birthing bed... a few hours later so did the baby girl she brought into the world. After my mother passed, my father was a broken man. There was nothing on this earth that he had ever loved except her... not even me. He had always been heavy-handed, but she had managed to temper him with her kindness."

Eilis said nothing. While she knew it must be difficult to recount these memories, she dared not interrupt him. This was obviously something that had been burdening him for some time, and she owed it to him to listen.

"My father took to drinking. If he was awake, there was a bottle or flask attached to his lips. It always put him in a piss poor mood, and I can't tell you how many times I had to help him home by half carrying and half dragging him from whatever brothel, tavern, or ditch he happened to pass out in."

Eilis saw a flash of pain in Albain's brown eyes, and he took a moment to compose himself before he could find the strength to continue his story. "Ale made him stupid; liquor made him mean. But when he took up drinking Rot Ale..." Albain shuddered at the memory. "Strong stuff; puts the devil in folk when they drink it, and my father already had enough of the devil in him. He started shouting at me for something I did or didn't do... I don't even remember what it was."

Albain ran his hand through his hair and met Eilis's eyes. "He got it in his head that I needed a good arse kicking, so he started wailing on me. I'd learned by then to just protect myself as much as I could, but I never dared to strike him back. By then, I was taller than he was, maybe even stronger, too, but I had nothing but fear for him in my heart, so I just stood there dumb as a doornail while he knocked out some of my teeth and cracked a few of my ribs.

"But things went from bad to worse quick. He picked up a wine bottle and started waving it around... smashed the end of the bottle on the table, leaving it sharp. He came at me, so I shoved him away. That just made him angrier."

Eilis wrapped her arms around him as he drew in a ragged breath.

"Some say that when you're about to die, time slows down. I remember everything from that night. I remember the feel of the glass scraping against my bone. I remember my back hitting the table in our common room as he drove the edge further into my face. I remember him telling me I was a waste of air, that I'd be better off dead, and that he cursed the Maker every night that my mother had died but I had lived. I remember the sour smell of wine on his breath. All of it. Every detail. It haunts my dreams sometimes, and I wake up soaked in sweat and sure as hell that he's in the room with me.

"There was a knife on the table. It was just within my reach. I did the only thing I could. I jammed it into his throat, and I watched him die. I could have tried to stop the bleeding or gone running for help... but I didn't. Been on my own ever since then, until... until you."

She hugged him even tighter, and he loved her for it. She pressed her cheek against his, and the feel of her skin against his brought some semblance of peace to the brimming emotion inside of him.

"I killed him."

"You had to."

"Aye. I did. Doesn't make it any easier though."

"How old were you?" asked Eilis softly.

"Fourteen. I buried him and left my clan's lands, though by then we were all that was left of the Cur. I took nothing, save for his sword, the one I still carry."

She took notice of the glistening of his eyes as he held back tears, the same ones he had been holding back his entire life.

"There are only two people alive who know that story." He looked at her meaningfully, and she knew it was with great trust that he had revealed the most vulnerable part of himself to her. "And now I've foolishly ruined our afternoon. I'm sorry... I should have—"

She silenced him with a kiss. "You've ruined nothing."

With her thumb, she traced the line of the scar on his face from the top of his forehead, down the side of his cheek, and to the base of his jawline.

"Albain, I am truly sorry for all that has befallen you."

"Don't be. It was worth it."

Eilis, unsure of his meaning, cocked her head slightly.

"It might have been hell on earth, but it was worth it. Every moment of pain, every scar, every sorrow... it led me to you." He pressed his forehead against hers and closed his eyes as he inhaled her scent, a subtle sweetness that reminded him of lilac.

His mouth sought out hers, and the instant he found it, he became overcome by his passion for her. Their kiss intensified, but she soon broke away and kissed the base of his neck, applying a delicate suck here and there, which sent his pulse racing. He pulled her tightly against his chest, and a moment later she was straddling him. His hands reached up to caress her breasts, and she resolved to remove the barrier between them, discarding her shirt upon the forest floor. He followed suit, leaving his bare chest exposed to the light of the sun that permeated the canopy of trees above them.

He sat up abruptly and pressed his lips against the gentle curve of her bosom. He became suddenly aware of the downward path of her hand, and his body gave an involuntary shudder when he felt her light touch upon him. She rocked back to her heels and parted from him, only to reach for his hands and bid him rise to his feet. Again, a jolt coursed through him as she felt him, and he was more than happy to oblige when she began to relieve him of his breeches. He stared at her in wonder as she hastily discarded her own, giving him full view of every inch of her flesh.

Now entirely naked, they found themselves exposed to a

crisp, autumn breeze. She looked like an angel from one of those paintings that adorned the walls of the Church of the Maker, and his breath caught in his throat as her hair briefly billowed behind her before once again falling to her shoulders as the soft wind died down again.

She seated herself on the earth and stretched out on the blanket. At first, he was completely rooted to the spot as he drank in the sight of her: every soft line and supple curve sent his mind reeling and his heart pounding.

She beckoned him to draw closer, and he knelt beside her. She placed her hand against the sharp bone of his hip, and he deftly maneuvered so that she rested beneath him. He settled himself between her thighs and patiently waited for some sign that she, indeed, wanted him there. She responded by shifting slightly, so that her woman's place just grazed the end of him.

He hesitated; a woman's virtue was a serious affair, and he knew that Eilis had remained untouched by any man. Despite her seeming consent, he still feared she may be unsure or would come to regret giving such a gift to someone like him.

As if reading his thoughts, she said, "I'm certain."

Mindful of her comfort, with all the gentleness he could command, he found himself within her. She gave a slight gasp when he had filled her with his entirety, and he ceased his movements until she gave a nod for him to continue. He moved back and forth slowly, luxuriating in the feel of her warmth around him.

Propping himself up on his hands, he leaned down and pressed his lips to hers as he delved deeper into her woman's place. She raised her hips to meet him, encouraging him to continue. Their bodies fell into a rhythm, and he fought to contain himself.

He had heard the jesting of men of Allanon, men like Ser Romley, who bragged about their conquests and cared nothing for the pleasure of their women, but Bromus men were far more mindful of the needs of their ladies.

Albain quickly learned how to best coax the satisfying sounds of gratification from Eilis, and only when he felt her claim her pleasure, her cheeks flushed and her inner place tightening around him, did he allow himself his own release.

An intense rush of euphoria washed over them as they clung to one another in its wake. He pressed another hard kiss against her lips while his body trembled slightly from the force of their lovemaking.

Eilis let out a deep sigh of contentment, which brought a smile to the face of her lover, and Albain paused to, once again, admire the beauty of the woman before him. Gingerly and reluctantly, he retreated from within her.

Half-exhausted, yet somehow still exhilarated, Albain collapsed to his side and wrapped his arms around Eilis while whispering words of love to her.

CHAPTER 10

Over the next fortnight, Eilis was forced to endure the arduous task of pretending to be thrilled over the prospect of marrying a man she didn't love. She smiled as she was fitted for a dress that she was determined she would never wear and went through the motions of selecting an orchestra for a ceremony that would never occur.

While part of her worried that she was mistaken, and Selwyn truly was innocent of any wrongdoing, every day there seemed to be more signs of his true intentions. He was frequently called away by his council, and over breakfast one day he had made the mistake of leaving a supply list on his desk. A quick glance informed Eilis that the document accounted for a large quantity of weapons and goods to be sent to the eastern border.

Still, while the supply list had somewhat supported her suspicions, she had been unable to acquire any firm proof of his guilt, and it was becoming a constant source of frustration for her.

One day, she again beseeched Albain to accompany her to go horseback riding while Selwyn attended to more pressing matters. Luckily, Eilis knew the perfect destination for the ride; it was roughly two hours from the castle and was a spot they had by then visited several times.

As was his custom, Albain spread the blanket on the forest floor, and the two of them stretched out next to each other. They listened to the soothing sound of the waterfall as they quietly enjoyed each other's company.

Eilis lazily drew little patterns on Albain's chest with her fingers. "I can't wait to be rid of Callor's Rest. The longer I stay there, the more certain I am that something is amiss. Late last night, I was looking out my window when I saw a visitor approach the main gate. They let him in without a moment's pause, and he was met directly by Selwyn."

Albain shrugged. "Lord Callor meets with many people."

"But this was the first Talvair I've seen at the castle."

Albain sat up abruptly. His eyes grew wide with shock. "A Talvair?"

Eilis sat up next to him. "Yes. He departed promptly after their meeting."

"Are you certain?"

Eilis nodded. "As he dismounted, I saw his weapon. You've taught me a great deal about blades, and I've never heard of anyone who wasn't a Talvair carrying a Talvair blade."

"We need to act soon."

"I've been thinking on this. The tournament is our best advantage."

"Bloody hell! That still seems so far away!" lamented Albain.

"I know, but everyone will be there, which means the staff will be reduced in the castle. That may be our best opportunity to search for proof. If there is evidence of his deceit, it is sure to be in his quarters. I can't imagine he would want such information too far from his person."

"I hate him," said Albain bitterly.

"I know. I was worried you were going to kill him when you sparred with him."

"Thought about it," he confessed honestly. "Still thinking about it. And seeing you with him... I can't bear to see you with another man." He took a deep breath, unsure of how to put his feelings for her into words, and half terrified to lay his soul so bare. "You once asked me about my intentions for you, so here they are." He clasped her hands in his. "You may take as much of me or as little of me as you want. I'll stay beside you forever if that's your wish, simply as your protector, or if you wanted it..." She could see the nervousness in his expression, and in that moment, there was a certain vulnerability present in his eyes.

"What if... what if I wanted more?"

"Name it, then. No man, no matter how great, will ever be good enough for you. I'm sure as hell not good enough for you, but I've given you my life as your Bloodsworn, and I'd give you my life as your husband, too, if you willed it, though I know the All-Chieftain would sooner kill me than call me his kin."

Eilis placed her hand on his arm. "He'd have to go through me to get to you."

"My protector," teased Albain. "Maybe you should have been *my* Bloodsworn. You are skilled enough with a blade." He lovingly caressed her cheek with his hand. "You know I'm no good when it comes to pretty words, so I'll say it plainly. Marry me... Or don't, if it's not in your heart. No matter what you choose, I'm yours. My heart is yours and yours alone."

She saw it for what it was: a proposal. It wasn't as flowery as that of Lord Callor's, but somehow, it was infinitely more heartfelt coming from a hardened man such as Albain. To think she had affected him in such a way was exhilarating, and to know her affections were returned touched her heart in ways she hadn't thought possible.

"Yes."

The power of such a simple word brought them crashing together. They moved almost as one. A kiss upon her neck and a hand upon his bare chest. His mouth upon her lips, and his rough hands pressed against the exposed skin of her back. She traced the outline of each of his many battle scars with her fingers before pressing a gentle kiss to each one. Just how many he lost count of, but each time she did, it seemed to heal something that was broken within him.

Afterwards, their clothes were strewn about the forest floor as the sun set and the stars came into view. She lay pressed against him, the heat of his skin dispelling the chill of the air. He wrapped the blanket around them, and she rested her head upon his chest. Half-giddy with satisfaction and blissful exhaustion, she listened to the steady sound of his heartbeat. She raised her head to look at him and pressed a gentle kiss against the scarred ravine that covered half of his face. While others did everything they could to avoid looking at the hideous mark, Eilis seemed to pay it extra mindfulness, as if those light brushes of her lips could somehow dispel the anguish that had caused it.

CHAPTER 11

The weeks that followed were a blur of activity. Eilis found she had few moments to herself as much of her time was filled with Selwyn's company or planning the wedding ceremony. Eilis knew all this was pointless as she certainly did not intend to marry the lord, and even should he be proved innocent of treason —which she found unlikely—she was determined to find a way that the nuptials would never occur. Still, it was a necessity that she go through the motions and feign the excitement of an eager bride.

At times, she almost felt guilty, as it seemed Selwyn did have genuine affection for her. He was constantly sending her small gifts and often sought her out for walks in the garden or conversations in the library. He never pressed her for more affection than she allowed and was content to walk with her hand in hand or partake in the occasional kiss or lingering embrace. However, for Eilis, each one of these gestures felt like a betrayal to the one she truly loved.

Eilis took notice of the fact that Selwyn was far more attentive to Albain's presence as of late. Outwardly, the lord bore the warrior no ill will. He had even congratulated the Bloodsworn on besting him and lauded him for his skill in combat. What he felt inwardly was another matter. Eilis was cognizant of the way that the lord now kept a watchful eye on Albain, and he more frequently requested that the warrior stand guard in the hallway when he wished to be alone with Eilis.

Despite all of the commitments demanded of her, Eilis still found time to steal away with Albain. As often as possible, they ventured into the woods for quiet moments together. She explained this to Selwyn as her missing her home. She was unaccustomed to living in castles and missed the woods and all the elements of nature that the Bromus lands afforded her. While the lord wasn't overly fond of these excursions and even begged her to take additional guards, he found that it was futile to argue the point with her any further.

One day, after another afternoon of "horseback riding," Eilis managed to coax Albain into the ice-cold pool that gathered at the base of the waterfall. It was an unseasonably warm day for autumn, and she eagerly stripped off her garments and made her way into the pool as Albain, a smile upon his face, stared after her in admiration. He leaned against a tree and was content to silently appreciate her beauty, but she beckoned for him to follow suit, and he quickly disrobed and joined her.

He enveloped her in his embrace and lifted her in the water. She wrapped her legs around his waist and leaned her head against his chest. His heartbeat always seemed to increase in its music whenever she was around him.

"I love you."

He spoke so softly she had barely heard him. A small smile affected her features, and she leaned back in his arms. "And I love you."

"Just thought… thought that I'd mention it. I know that I don't get to say it as much as I'd like to… but I hope you know that I do."

She nodded. "I know."

"This is all… new for me. I never thought any woman would pay me mind, especially one like you. Didn't think I'd ever have… you know… all this."

It was one of several moments that succeeded in further strengthening the bond between them.

"Soon, we can go home. We can create a life together," she promised him.

Albain snorted. "I'm sure your grandfather will be thrilled."

Eilis shrugged. "He won't have a choice in the matter. I know the nature of my heart, and I won't be parted from you."

* * *

A few days before the celebration was scheduled to be held, Eilis was once again having breakfast with Selwyn in his chambers. It had become a daily ritual that the two of them dined together in the morning before taking a stroll around the grounds. There was a knock at the door, and moments later, a messenger entered the room with glad tidings.

"The All-Chieftain has arrived, and we received word that the King and Prince Trystan are expected to arrive tomorrow."

Eilis excitedly leapt from her chair, which elicited a chuckle from Selwyn who quickly followed her from the room. Albain trailed a few steps behind them.

Eilis, with the unbridled glee of a child, bounded into her grandfather's arms and nearly toppled them both the ground. "Granda!"

"My dear girl!" The All-Chieftain chuckled at her emphatic greeting and kissed the crown of his granddaughter's head. "You look as strong as ever." He held her at an arm's length. "And even more beautiful than last I saw you. There's a... a glow about you. I hear happiness does that to a woman in love. At least it did for your grandmother, Maker rest her soul."

Once her grandfather had the opportunity to rest, Eilis came to him in his chambers and told him all that she had witnessed since her arrival. He listened with rapt attention, and when she concluded her tale, his reaction was equal parts concern and rage.

"I should have bloody well known better than to trust these fool royals!" he roared.

"Shh!" Eilis put her hand on his forearm to calm him.

"We need proof before all hell breaks loose!"

"Albain and I have a plan, but we can't act on it until the day of the tournament. The king will be here by then. If Lord Callor is guilty, I have a notion of where he may have put anything documenting his alliance with the Talvair."

Her grandfather agreed with her evaluation, and there was nothing they could do but wait for the right time to act.

CHAPTER 12

The following evening, Lord Callor received word that the King and his company had reached the edge of town. Selwyn rode out to meet them, and while he and the king progressed at a leisurely pace, Prince Trystan and his personal guard rode ahead.

Immediately upon arriving at Callor's Rest, Trystan sought out Eilis, as she anticipated he would. She opened the door to her chambers before he even had the opportunity to knock. Trystan, followed by his bodyguard, a young woman by the name of Rose, quickly entered the room.

Rose was a bit of a curiosity and an unlikely candidate for the trusted position of personal bodyguard to the heir of Allanon. She and the prince had first met while she was a prisoner in the dungeon. Rose had been imprisoned for stealing a prized heirloom from the royal family and incapacitating over a dozen guards in her attempt to escape.

While King Ruden had been incensed by her brazen crime, the prince had been intrigued as to how a young, slender woman with no armor and a dagger had managed to outmatch so many trained and heavily armed guards. Trystan had been struck by Rose's intelligence, cunning, and skill, and instead of having her executed, he had given her a job, much to the king's displeasure.

Despite the fact that Rose had a bit of an edge to her, a quality that many perceived as rude or even openly hostile, Eilis found her blunt honesty rather refreshing, and the two had struck up a friendship. Since coming into the prince's employment, Rose had accompanied Trystan on his yearly pilgrimage to the Bromus lands. Every year, Eilis went to Vericus to visit the prince, and he returned the gesture in kind by going to see Eilis and her kin. Rose was always a welcome addition. She enjoyed the camaraderie to be found among the clans, and even the All-Chieftain had expressed the sentiment that she was welcome among them at any time.

"All right, Eilis. What's going on?" Trystan demanded as he crossed his arms over his chest.

Albain, seated in a plush armchair, exchanged glances with Rose and gestured for her to follow him to the hallway. "Best to leave these two to talk."

As soon as their protectors left the room, Trystan looked at Eilis expectantly.

"Trystan, believe me when I say that I wish I could tell you—"

"Fantastic, I wish for you to tell me as well. However, I know you well enough to know that there is a *but* coming, and I'm likely not going to get an answer to my question."

"I want to, Trystan, but I'm going to have to ask you to trust me for just a while longer."

"It's about Selwyn, isn't it? I knew you wouldn't be foolish enough to marry that cox-comb."

Eilis sighed. "Well, you're not wrong. It does have to do with Lord Callor, but I can't move forward until I find the proof that I need. There is a great deal at risk. Trystan, I'm going to need you to trust me. Hopefully, I'm wrong, and there will be nothing to discuss... but if I'm right..."

"Say no more," replied Trystan. "Eilis, we've been best friends since we were children. In fact, you're more like a sister to me than a friend. I would trust you with my life. If you need to maintain your secrecy, then I won't press you any further on the matter. It's enough for me just to hear you haven't lost your mind and truly fallen for my imbecile cousin."

"You've *nothing* to worry about on that matter."

There was a knock at the door, and Albain briefly popped his head into the room. "You're being summoned for dinner. Best we get going."

Rose, too, poked her head into the room. "Thank the Maker! I'm starving! Come on, your highness. I spied a servant downstairs with a plate of honeycakes. I need them in my life immediately."

"We'll be out in a moment," said Trystan.

Albain and Rose disappeared from view, and Trystan closed the distance between himself and Eilis, wrapping her in a firm embrace.

"There. Now that we've got all that out of the way, I've got to tell you that I've missed you, Eilis. I haven't seen you since before Maker's Day. Beyond this madness, how have you been faring?"

"Beyond this, exceptionally well. Trystan, so much has happened! There's so much that I want to tell you."

Trystan smirked and carefully scrutinized her expression. "Does it have anything to do with that Bloodsworn of yours?"

Eilis blanched, caught off guard by his remark. "Wh-what?"

"Don't think I haven't noticed the way you two are always stealing glances at one another."

"Trystan, that's a rather bold proclamation to make after having only been here for less than twenty minutes."

"Please," replied Trystan. "I was there when he offered himself as your Bloodsworn."

It was true; the prince had been visiting with the Oak Clan when Albain had declared his intention to serve as Eilis's lifelong protector.

"And I've had the occasion to see you two together several times since then. You can't deny what's as plain as day."

Eilis sighed. "Just how *plain* is it, Trystan?"

"Plain enough that your best friend would notice, but not plain enough that anyone else would likely catch wind of it. So, I was right? That's what has happened?"

Eilis nodded, and the prince grinned in satisfaction.

"Don't think you're so guarded, Trystan. I'd wager you and Rose have done quite a bit more than kissing under an apple tree," teased Eilis.

"I never should have told you about that," muttered Trystan. "A fine pair we make. My father is still trying to convince me to marry Princess Marina of Blackwood, but my heart has been stolen by an *actual* thief. And you... you've fallen for a man who could probably take down an entire army by himself."

Eilis couldn't help but to be amused by the strange and difficult situations that she and her friend had found themselves in. "I'll be lucky if Granda doesn't try to kill Albain when I finally get around to telling him."

"Maker willing, my father will just disown me. I don't really want to be king anyway. Might the Oak Clan have a need for an exiled royal?" joked Trystan as he offered Eilis his arm.

"For you, I'm sure we can make some sort of arrangement." She looped her arm through his and allowed him to accompany her to dinner.

❊ ❊ ❊

As they all gathered around the massive table in the great hall, King Ruden gave his formal blessing for the union of his nephew and Eilis of the Oak Clan. Lord Callor pushed to have the marriage contract signed immediately, but the All-Chieftain deflected the request, saying he wished to review the terms more closely before consenting for his granddaughter to be wed. Reluctantly, Lord Callor conceded.

The rest of the evening was filled with enough food and drink to feed all of Allanon. Ser Romley, who had partaken of far more wine than he should have, loudly boasted of the matches that would be held at the tournament. Many illustrious warriors would be partaking in the events. Lord Callor had insisted that Albain participate. Despite the latter's refusal as he stated he had a vow to uphold as Eilis's Bloodsworn, the All-Chieftain had given Albain leave to participate in the tournament to "show them all the might of the Bromus."

CHAPTER 13

On the day of the tournament, King Ruden and the All-Chieftain, made their way to the tournament grounds while Lord Callor, Eilis, Prince Trystan, and their respective guards lingered a short distance behind.

"I left something at the castle," Eilis said to Selwyn.

"What is it? I'll have a servant retrieve it for you."

"My favorite shawl, the one you gifted me. I wanted to wear it today. You said it looked fetching."

"You are a vision of beauty." Selwyn embraced his betrothed. "How could you even become any more radiant than you already are?"

"For you, I'll find a way." She feigned delight, and Albain wondered how the lord could not hear the counterfeit nature of her emotions. "I know exactly where it is. It will be faster if I get it."

"Very well. I know better than to interfere with a woman's will to look her best." Selwyn leaned in to claim a kiss from Eilis, an action that never ceased in making Albain want to slit the noble's throat.

"You go on. I'll join you soon," she assured him.

"Be not long, my dear," the lord called after her. "The first match will begin soon. I want you by my side when I open the tournament."

"Yes, don't be long, Eilis," echoed Trystan with a meaningful look to her and Albain. The prince still wasn't sure what was going on, but it was evident he was eager to find out.

Lord Callor, Prince Trystan, and Rose continued on while Albain and Eilis made their way back to the castle.

Once they were satisfied the nobles would not be promptly returning, they made their way to Lord Callor's chambers. There were two guards stationed just outside his door, but Eilis had already anticipated this.

"Good day, Roland," greeted Eilis smilingly.

The larger of the two guards beamed at her as she approached. "Good day, Lady Eilis." A look of confusion passed over his face. "I thought my lord had already departed for the tourney."

"He has. I joined him for breakfast this morning, and in doing so, left my favorite shawl therein," explained Eilis. "He gave me leave to come collect it before rejoining him. There's a chill to the air today and he said he would be most distraught if I were to catch cold so close to our nuptials."

The other guard eyed her warily. "No one is to enter the lord's chambers without his consent."

"As I have said, he has already given his consent," reminded Eilis sweetly.

Roland moved to open the door to allow her entry, but the other guard still seemed reluctant.

Eilis continued the charade. "If you'd like—Jessup, is it?"

The other guard nodded.

"You may send a messenger to go and confirm such with Lord Callor, but doing so will further delay me joining him," reasoned Eilis. "He said the first match will be starting soon and that it is imperative that I be by his side when the tournament begins, as the reason for it is to celebrate our impending marriage."

"You'll make a lovely bride," commented Roland cheerily.

"Thank you so much for saying so, Roland." She leaned forward and spoke to him conspiratorially but still loud enough for the other guard to hear. "I'll make it my personal goal to ensure that you're no longer put on the late watch."

Roland bowed. "My lady, you are far too kind."

"Very well," relented Jessup. "I've no desire to anger our lord by delaying you. Just be quick about it." He opened the door wide for Eilis. "And when you're determining watches, be sure to remember Jessup, too."

"Of course, Jessup," agreed Eilis. She turned to her Bloodsworn. "You may remain here, Albain."

He bowed slightly at her command.

"I am sure I have no need for you to guard me within, especially with such excellent men keeping my lord's chambers safe," charmed Eilis.

Roland closed the door behind her, and Eilis moved directly to Selwyn's study. There was a very fine desk in the center of the room, but upon studying the lord and his habits, Eilis knew she wouldn't find what she was looking for there.

Instead, she crossed to his bookshelf and selected the largest volume.

Mathematics.

She opened the book and found what she had suspected she might find. This book had been selected for his shelf specifically because it was *not* one he enjoyed. A box had been cut in the pages to form an area in which the lord could hide papers in plain sight. Of course he wouldn't defile one of his precious tomes in such a way! He would only be able to do so to a book for which he had no regard.

Eilis quickly rifled through the papers until she found what she was looking for: two separate documents bearing Lord Callor's seal. One was an agreement of allegiance, and in addition to Lord Callor's seal was the signature of Bagatur Gunari, the leader of the Talvair. The Talvair were indeed under the command of Lord Callor. That must also have been why they had not recently moved further into Bromus lands. Selwyn had likely ordered them not to out of respect for his relationship with Eilis. She did not doubt that Selwyn intended to use both the Talvair and the Bromus to decimate the royal army of King Ruden.

The second document was the most damning. It was a treaty signed by both Lord Callor and King Ulric McGairn of Evinster. A brief glance at the treaty revealed that King Ulric would support Lord Callor's claim to the throne due to his father having been the intended King of Allanon by birthright. He also agreed to a formal alliance between the two countries.

Eilis reddened considerably as she read the final clause of the agreement. Selwyn pledged that upon becoming king, he would concede ¼ of the holdings of Allanon to King Ulric as payment for his assistance. Coincidentally, the holdings described were all Bromus lands.

She carefully replaced the book just as Selwyn had positioned it then tucked the documents into the front of her dress. She then grabbed her shawl from beneath the table where she had deliberately placed it during breakfast. She wrapped it around her shoulders and hurried from the room.

"I found it!" she exclaimed as she exited. "Come, Albain. We must go with haste. My beloved awaits." She turned back to the guards, thanking them again for their assistance, then hurried off with Albain.

Once they were out of earshot of the guards, Albain inquired about her search. "Did you manage to find what we were looking for?"

Eilis nodded gravely. "It's worse than we thought." She explained the contents of the documents to Albain who looked as if he desired nothing more than to tear Lord Callor limb from limb.

His words came out as a growl. "He'd give our lands to King Ulric as payment for being party to his treason? Stupid cunt. I should have broken more than his arm."

They reached the tournament grounds just in time. Before Eilis was ushered to the royal viewing box, she took Albain aside.

"I have something for you," she whispered to him.

He eyed her curiously.

She reached to the back of her neck and unclasped the silver chain that had graced her neck nearly all of her life. "I want to give you my favor. Here. Bend down."

He did as she bid him. "Favors," he snorted. "A Bromus warrior prancing around like some bloody Allanon knight." She placed the chain around his neck and clasped it in the back.

"It's a custom that men take a favor from their ladies in tourneys. Am I not your lady?"

"Aye, that you are." He bent down again, as if to whisper something in her ear, but slyly pressed a kiss against the side of her neck, an action that always seemed to elicit a pleasurable sensation in his beloved.

A chill ran down Eilis's spine. "You're wicked."

"You're worse," he returned. "You don't know the things you do to me. Now get on with you. Your *lord* awaits."

She frowned at his words, but he only grinned before shaking his head in amusement and lumbering off in the direction of the area that had been allotted for the combatants to prepare.

Upon seeing Eilis arrive, Selwyn rose to his feet and quickly took her hand in his. He pressed a chaste kiss to her cheek and again complimented her beauty. While Prince Trystan looked positively disgusted, King Ruden was elated to see his favorite kinsmen so taken by Eilis, though his glee was sure to be short-lived.

Lord Callor gave the dedication of the tourney, all the while lauding the strength and skill of the warriors and reminding them of the cause for the celebration, as well as the considerable sum of money that the winner of the tourney would receive.

As they seated themselves, Eilis squeezed her grandfather's hand and offered a reassuring smile as if to tell him they had found what they needed. There was a look of relief upon his face, and he nodded in silent acknowledgment. They had agreed that any information Eilis found would be exchanged after the tournament as doing so during could lead to chaos. Approaching King Ruden with the information while there could lead Lord Callor to take drastic actions, and as the All-Chieftain wanted to neither endanger themselves nor the king, he had suggested they wait until after the tournament had concluded and the All-Chieftain had the opportunity to approach the king without his nephew present.

* * *

There were many thrilling matches in the tournament. Ser Romley did reasonably well in his first match, but he was defeated in his second match by Ser Adric Thorne. Albain managed to best some of the most skilled knights that Allanon offered. He decimated Ser Morgan and made quick work of Ser Keats. Ser Bael proved to be more of a challenge, but he too was defeated by Albain's superior speed and strength. Finally, much to Eilis's delight, only her Bloodsworn and Lord Callor's champion, Ser Koth Pembrell remained.

Next to Albain himself, Ser Koth was the largest man she had ever seen. While Albain was certainly strong and well-muscled, Ser Koth looked like one of the stone giants of legend. His immense frame was covered in heavy, steel plate armor, but his strength was such that he seemed entirely unencumbered. He was slower than Albain, but his blows seemed more fearsome. The living titan had rendered all of his foes unconscious in their bouts, and one of them was rumored to have sustained a possibly fatal head injury. Despite Eilis's confidence in her Bloodsworn, she feared for Albain's safety against such a brute.

During the joust, Albain had the advantage and managed to unseat Ser Koth on the second pass. Ser Koth scrambled to his feet and hefted his greatsword into his hands. Like Albain, he declined fighting with a broadsword and shield in favor of the raw power that the larger weapon afforded.

Albain glanced towards the royal viewing box. He caught sight of Eilis, whose face shone with pride for the success of her beloved. Then, he saw something that filled him with incomparable rage. Selwyn was turned in his seat, more focused on Eilis than the match before him. One of his hands rested on her shoulder, while the other rested on her thigh. The lord leaned over to whisper something in her ear before begging another kiss from her.

Albain thought of the silver chain that now hung around his neck. It was *her* favor, for him and him alone. Meanwhile, Lord Callor was willing to betray not only the Bromus, but his own king and people. He did not deserve the smallest measure of Eilis's attention, even if it was false.

Albain let out a roar as he closed the distance between himself and Ser Koth. The thrill of combat coursed through his body, and the instant he found himself within range of Lord Callor's champion, he exploded towards his opponent and began a relentless assault of flashing steel. Albain was a whirlwind of well-placed, punishing blows that left Ser Koth constantly on the defense. The Bromus warrior pounded against the knight's chest and hit him so hard in the shoulder that his pauldron flew off his body and careened several yards across the field.

It looked as if Albain would make short work of the knight, but the warrior realized his folly too late. The knight was toying with him and testing the strength of the Bloodsworn's blows. It wasn't long before Albain found himself on the defense. A punishing slam to his helm made his ears ring and his vision swirl. A sweep to his knees left him scrambling to right himself from the dirt. When Ser Koth swung his greatsword towards Albain's chest, the Bromus quickly tried to dodge out of the way but did not manage to wholly escape the blow. The wind was robbed from his lungs, and he struggled to catch his breath before renewing his own attack.

"Get him, Albie! Kick his arse!" came a voice from the crowd.

Albain smirked as he caught sight of Lark and his father in the stands.

"Lark!" exclaimed Sebastian.

"Sorry, Da."

Albain felt reinvigorated; he'd give the kid a fight worth watching.

The two giants exchanged blow for blow, and the once cheering audience was reduced to anxious and awestruck silence as the opponents continued to hammer on each other with all their might.

Finally, Albain took advantage of an opening in Ser Koth's attack, and it allowed him to get the upper hand. He managed to get behind Ser Koth and brought his sword down with all the strength he could muster. Lord Callor's champion collapsed to his stomach from the force of the blow, and Albain planted his boot on the knight's back to indicate that in battle this would have given him the opportunity for a deathblow.

The small Bromus portion of the crowd erupted in loud cheers while the rest of the onlookers were soon compelled to admit their appreciation for the Bloodsworn as well.

Resounding horns marked the end of the tournament and commanded the attention of the audience to the viewing box at the end of the field.

Lord Callor stood therein. There was a broad smile on his face, and he kept a hand on Eilis's shoulder as he spoke. "Good people of Callor's Rest, our esteemed guests, and our most beloved king! I present to you, the champion of this most blessed matrimonial tournament! Albain of the Bromus! The fearsome Cur!"

The crowd roared in approval, but Albain didn't care for their regard or Lord Callor's hollow words. Instead, his gaze was fixed on Eilis, whose expression beamed with pride over her lover's performance and excitement at the prospect of leaving Callor's Rest. Albain could practically hear her thoughts.

"Soon. We can go home. We can finally be together."

The idea of finally having Eilis to himself—provided the All-Chieftain didn't end him immediately upon learning of their intentions—was enough to coax a smile from the Bloodsworn. Eilis had assured him her grandfather would be swayed when she told him of how loyally he had protected and served her and how instrumental Albain had been in their efforts to uncover Lord Callor's plot.

Lord Callor beckoned Albain forward and awarded him with his winnings, an impressive amount of gold.

"Well-done, Albain! Well-done!" congratulated the All-Chieftain. "Knew that none of these pompous knights could hold their own against a real warrior!"

Albain put his fist over his heart and gave a slight bow of acknowledgment in response to the All-Chieftain's words.

Albain, anxious to rejoin Eilis, took his leave. He returned to the arming area to gather his belongings and entered the tent where he had prepared for his bout. He took off his plate armor as it was in need of some repair and changed into his studded, leather jerkin and a fresh pair of trousers. A grand feast was to follow the tournament, but Albain guessed that much of the evening's activities would be upended once details of Lord Callor's treachery came to light.

As he bent to grab his cloak, from behind him, he heard the heavy thud of footsteps. Albain whirled around to face the interloper.

Ser Koth stood a few feet away from him. "I came to congratulate you on your win. Not many best me in combat."

"I admit you're strong. You almost had me a few times. You were the best challenge I've had in years."

"You are a worthy foe." Ser Koth extended his hand to Albain who, after a moment's hesitation, took it.

A strange expression passed over the knight's face, something akin to regret.

Suddenly, Albain felt a searing pain in his stomach. He cried out in agony and glanced down at his abdomen to search for the cause of his turmoil. Blood poured over the grip of a dagger that had been embedded in his gut. His eyes widened with surprise, and he staggered forward.

Ser Koth pulled the dagger free as Albain clutched at his belly and slumped to the ground.

As a warrior, Albain had been stabbed many times in his life, and he'd even had more grievous wounds than this. However, he noted the way his vision swam, and the wound seemed to burn unnaturally. It took him mere seconds to realize that he had been poisoned.

Albain cursed his own foolishness. He had completely disregarded one of his own tenets: trust no one. Typically, he would have been more cautious, even when confronted by a well-wisher. Years of being on his own had taught him to view kind acts and honeyed words with suspicion. However, he had been so distracted by the prospect of finally leaving Callor's Rest and enjoying a proper life with his beloved that he had carelessly let his guard down, and now he would pay dearly for his mistake.

"I have no quarrel with you," spoke Ser Koth sincerely. "Quite frankly, I had hoped for a rematch. I was earnest when I said you were a worthy foe. You have my respect."

Albain groaned and attempted to pull himself to his feet

A familiar voice emanated from the opening of the tent. "No, the quarrel is mine. The mighty Cur... as strong as ten men... felled by a measly dagger. Shameful really."

Ser Romley appeared in Albain's view. He promptly slammed his knee into the warrior's chest and caused him to falter again. With a smile of satisfaction, he knelt beside Albain as the warrior again tried to struggle to his feet, but to no avail. "Go, Koth. Leave me to this. The Cur is no danger to me. He is a dog without teeth."

The massive knight lingered at the entrance of the tent for a moment but soon disappeared from view.

"What? You thought my brother would continue to endure the way you look at his betrothed? Your interest is far more involved than that of a mere protector. It was Lady Gismene who figured it out. At first, we thought her accusations were merely the result of a jealous woman who had been turned away, but she was insistent that there was something to be wary of, and we now see that she was right. You love Lady Eilis. While I truly doubt she would ever show any true affection for you, we know she trusts you, and we can't risk you distracting her from her loyalty to my brother."

Suddenly, Ser Romley's eyes narrowed as he noticed something glistening in the fading sunlight. "Wait a moment..." He reached down and grabbed the thin, silver chain around Albain's neck. He gave it a hard tug, snapping the clasp and removing it from Albain. "This belongs to Lady Eilis. Is this a favor? Did she give this to you?"

Albain tried to snatch the necklace from Ser Romley's grasp, but the latter only laughed as he rose to his feet and slammed his boot into Albain's stomach, causing the warrior to let out another cry of agony.

Ser Romley turned his back on the fallen Bloodsworn. "I'd say it's nothing personal, but I won't lie to a dying man."

Albain called upon what was left of his rapidly fading strength. He managed to haul himself to his knees, but he couldn't catch his breath, and his body would no longer obey his commands. His chest heaved, and his vision swam. He succumbed to the blackness well before his body hit the ground.

CHAPTER 14

As soon as the tournament ended, Eilis took her grandfather aside and gave him the evidence that would prove Lord Callor's guilt. While the Lord of Callor's Rest was engaged in conversation with one of his kinsmen, the All-Chieftain promptly approached King Ruden.

"Might I have a word with you?" he entreated the monarch. "I had hoped to speak with you about a matter of some urgency."

Selwyn, overhearing this, said, "Nothing awful, I hope. I have heard of the difficulties your people have been enduring with the Talvair."

Eilis bristled at the comment but managed to bite her tongue and keep her composure.

"No, no. Nothing you need to be concerned with, Lord Callor," diverted the All-Chieftain.

Lord Callor approached Eilis and took her hands in his own. "I hope you will forgive me, my darling. I must go find my brother. It seems I owe him a considerable sum. We made a friendly wager prior to the tournament, and it seems his confidence in your Bloodsworn's abilities was superior to my belief in my own champion. I shall see you in the great hall for supper." He quickly pressed a kiss to her cheek before disappearing from the viewing box.

Eilis was left alone with Prince Trystan and Rose to await Albain's return.

However, when some time had passed and he still did not arrive, Eilis began to grow concerned.

Prince Trystan took notice of this and attempted to assuage her worries. "Perhaps he is delayed. Every knight in Callor's Rest probably wanted to praise him for his victory. That was no easy match!"

Eilis frowned. "Delayed? No, not Albain. He's my Bloodsworn; he hates to leave me unguarded."

Rose snickered. "I'm sure that's not the only reason he hates to be apart from you."

Eilis gave Trystan a stern look. "You told her?"

Trystan simply raised his hands before him. "It may have come up in conversation. I simply told her I thought that you and Albain were a good match."

"It's not as if it was news to me anyway," remarked Rose. "Last time we visited your people, Dennan, Ragnar, and I made a wager about it. It seems the wolf and the bear owe me some gold."

Eilis sighed at the mention of two of her close friends, Dennan of the Wolf Clan and Ragnar of the Bear Clan. "It seems like everyone is benefitting from wagers today," muttered Eilis.

"Betting against Albain," scoffed Trystan. "I told you Selwyn was an idiot."

Eilis turned to depart. "I'm going to go look for Albain. It is unlike him to be gone for so long."

"Very well. We'll accompany you," offered Trystan. "Besides, I'd like to offer my congratulations to him as well."

They made their way to the arming area on the west side of the tournament grounds. There, those who had participated in the tourney were collecting their belongings, cleaning their weapons, and tending to repairs on their armor. Eilis knew that Albain preferred to be left alone and did not like to be bothered by the mindless prattle of others when he prepared for combat, so she made her way to a lone tent on the far side of the area.

As she suspected, his immense, black warhorse was tethered outside. The beast appeared somewhat distressed, and upon seeing Eilis began to whinny incessantly.

"Albain?" Eilis called out.

There was no reply.

"Perhaps you should go in and check. Make sure he's decent before the rest of us head in," teased Rose with a suggestive wink to Eilis.

Trystan laughed loudly, and Eilis gave them both a sharp look of reproof.

"Albain?" Eilis called again as she entered the tent.

She had never known true fear until that moment.

Her beloved lay upon his back in the center of the tent. Blood poured from a grave wound in his abdomen. She rushed forward and knelt beside him as she frantically cried his name.

Hearing Eilis's distress, Trystan, Rose and several of the prince's guards hurried into the tent.

"Eilis, what's going on?" asked Trystan, his voice frantic with worry.

"He's been attacked. Someone go get a healer. Hurry!" she shouted.

One of the guards dashed from the tent to get help while Eilis immediately set to tending to the wound. She hastily opened his jerkin and pulled up the blood-soaked shirt beneath. She grabbed Albain's cloak from nearby and pressed it to the wound in an attempt to slow the bleeding.

"Who could have done this?" wondered Trystan aloud.

"A coward," returned Eilis. "It's not just the wound. Albain is strong; he could endure that alone." She briefly lifted the cloak, just long enough to get another look at the wound. She saw the blue spiderwebs that emanated from the wound, their point of origin. "He's been poisoned."

"Poisoned?" asked Rose.

"Yes, I'm quite certain. Nighthollow. Where is that bloody healer! Trystan, tell one of your guards to send word that Morning Bell will be needed. It will counteract the poison."

One of the royal guards was about to depart when Rose spoke. "Don't bother."

"What?" asked Eilis in confusion.

"You needn't send for it." She reached into her shoulder bag and began to search through the contents therein. Within seconds she held a small vial filled with a thick, purple liquid. She handed it to Eilis who, recognizing it as Morning Bell extract, set to administering it to her beloved.

"I'm afraid to ask, but how is it you just happen to have an antidote for poison on you?" questioned Trystan.

Rose shrugged. "So if I accidentally cut myself when I poison my blades, I don't die."

"You poison your blades?" cried Trystan in alarm.

"Why do you seem so surprised?" returned Rose casually. "Such things are common knowledge in my line of work."

After what seemed like an eternity, several healers arrived and set to work on stabilizing Albain.

"That was quick thinking on your part," one of them said to Eilis. "Had the Morning Bell been administered any later, he wouldn't have a chance at all. I don't want to give you false hope; I can't promise you that he will live. However, his heart remains strong."

Eilis prayed that the Maker would give him the strength he needed to return to her. Her mind began to wonder over who could have done this to Albain.

"Perhaps it was a robbery. He just received the tournament winnings," suggested Trystan.

Rose shook her head. "No. The gold's still here." She gestured to the heavy, leather pouch that lay near Albain's armor.

Eilis glanced around the tent, and just near where one of the guards had previously been standing were two sets of footprints unlike the rest. Eilis's grandfather had taught her tracking among many other skills, and she was particularly observant when it came to prints. She took note of the size of the footprints in the soft mud around where Albain had been found. Among those left by the healers, the guards, Eilis herself, Trystan, and Rose, there were two more sets that bore distinct patterns.

One seemed to be made by a pair of fine leather boots of average size. However, the other set looked as if it had been made by a giant. Eilis knew they did not belong to Albain as they were distinctly wider than his. However, she knew of one other man who was large enough to leave behind such massive tracks. They could only belong to Ser Koth.

Perhaps Lord Callor's champion had been embarrassed by his defeat and sought vengeance upon his opponent. However, Eilis's instincts told her it was not so simple. The other set of tracks was a concern, and there was the fact that, as Lord Callor's favored knight, Ser Koth stood to lose a great deal were he to be implicated in such a crime. Such a man would not have foolishly thrown away a position of great respect and wealth so easily.

Unless he had more to gain.

Only people who wanted their victims to suffer would dare to use poison, especially one as potent as Nighthollow, known to cause intense and debilitating pain. Whoever did this wanted Albain to suffer, and Eilis's instincts told her there was one person who would benefit more than any other if Albain were to die.

"Lord Callor," muttered Eilis under her breath.

"What?" asked Trystan from beside her.

"He went to find his brother, Ser Romley, right after the tournament. He said he owed him a debt, but I don't think it was from the wager as he had said. He wanted to see if he carried out the attack. The smaller prints could be from Ser Romley's boots. They are well-made and likely be a match. The larger prints must be Ser Koth's."

"You think my cousin tried to have Albain killed?" asked Trystan in disbelief.

Eilis let out a heavy sigh. "His treachery goes far beyond this, Trystan."

One of the healers called for a cart to transport Albain back to the castle.

"Seek out my grandfather when we return to the castle," Eilis said to the prince. "He'll tell you everything."

Albain was carefully loaded into the cart, and Eilis took up a position beside him. She clasped his hand in her own. It was still warm to the touch, which brought her some measure of hope. She knew the tenacity of her beloved, and she was sure he would never leave her without a fight.

When they reached the castle, they were immediately informed by one of the All-Chieftain's men that Lord Callor and

Ser Romley had been called into a meeting with King Ruden and the All-Chieftain. While this brought Eilis some satisfaction, she was too concerned for Albain's well-being to take proper pleasure in the downfall of a traitor.

Once the healers had done all they could, Eilis sent word of Albain's condition to her grandfather and asked that Prince Trystan relate her suspicions regarding the part Ser Romley and Ser Koth had played in the attack.

Within the hour, Lord Selwyn Callor and his brother, Ser Romley, were confined to the dungeons on charges of treason, and Ser Koth, who had been attempting to quietly flee the castle, was apprehended for the attempt on Albain's life.

* * *

That evening, Eilis passed the entire night by her Bloodsworn's side. There was a soft knock upon the door followed by Trystan's familiar voice. She bid him enter, and he and Rose made their way into the room.

"Eilis... I just wanted to say that I'm so very sorry. Your grandfather told me everything. I knew Selwyn was a prat, but this... I never in a million years would have thought he could do something so awful. Had I suspected any of this, I would have fought my father all the more about having you sent here."

Eilis raised her eyes and saw the genuine regret in the prince's expression. "You couldn't have known, Trystan. Selwyn had many people fooled."

"I wish you would have told me sooner... that I could have helped somehow."

"Believe me; I wanted to tell you what was going on the instant my suspicions took root. It was difficult to keep it from you. However, treason is a serious allegation, and it would have reflected poorly upon my people if my suspicions were unfounded. You know that. We couldn't risk your father somehow finding out before we were sure, especially since Selwyn was one of his favorites."

Rose snorted. "Not anymore."

"I, for one, am glad to be rid of that idiot and his repugnant brother," growled Trystan. "They were would-be usurpers of the throne, and had their plan succeeded, there is a good chance my father and I would be dead. It seems Selwyn would have gone to any lengths to reclaim what he thought was his birthright. Allanon is indebted to you... and your Bloodsworn. I am heartily sorry for what has befallen him. Albain is a good man, and I know that he brings you a great deal of happiness."

"We're to be wed," replied Eilis quietly.

Trystan and Rose exchanged a look of surprise, and the prince moved towards Eilis. He offered his hand to her and pulled her to her feet before enveloping her in a brotherly embrace.

"You had said things had progressed between the two of you, but I had not guessed it was to such a degree. I'll pray to the Maker that he is returned to you and can fulfill the vow he promised you."

"Thank you, Trystan."

He and Rose stayed for some time, neither of them wanting to leave Eilis alone to her grief. However, as the night wore on, Eilis noticed the prince was having a great deal of difficulty keeping his eyes open, so she bid him to retire for the evening. Despite her insistence that she would be fine, it was with great reluctance that Trystan and Rose departed.

Eilis wouldn't allow herself to rest her eyes for even a moment. Instead, she focused on the labored sound of Albain's breaths. She knew that if they ceased, her world would be undone, and all her dreams for the future would die along with him.

Alone, she prayed to the Maker to spare the man she loved.

* * *

The next few days were a blur. King Ruden was earnest in his profuse apologies to the All-Chieftain and his granddaughter over all that had transpired, but a million condolences could not bring Albain back from the brink of death. Only time and prayers that the healing measures proved successful could do that.

For Eilis's part, she never left Albain's side, and her grandfather began to worry for her well-being.

One evening, he sat down beside her, unsure of what he could say to rouse her from her sorrow. He placed his hand upon her shoulder as a gesture of comfort and spoke softly to her.

"I pray for his recovery, but Eilis, you must know how grave this looks. There is a strong possibility that he may not... that he may not come back to us."

She knew her grandfather did not mean to cause her pain; his words were meant to prepare her for the possibility that Albain may not live. However, the very thought of a world without him was enough to nearly reduce her to tears.

So much of her future happiness rested on the wounded man in the bed before her. As of late, her mind had often wandered to what the coming years could bring. She would truly be his, and he would be hers. No longer would they have to skulk about in the shadows, shielding their love from prying eyes, and when the day came that Eilis would become All-Chieftain, she would do so with her Bloodsworn, her beloved, by her side.

Now, with each ragged breath he drew, her world swayed on a precarious precipice; she could do nothing but wait and see which way it fell.

Her grandfather studied her for several moments before wrapping a brawny arm around her shoulders. "I see it, you know."

"See what?" asked Eilis, fighting back tears.

"You love him," he said softly. "In truth, I had thought it might bloom if left unattended."

Eilis did not even attempt to deny it. "I do, Granda. I love him with all my being." She was silent for a moment as she considered something he had said. "You say you thought it might happen, that something could bloom between us; yet, you didn't intervene."

"As if I could!" he exclaimed. "I know you, Eilis. I raised you to be strong and independent, and while upon occasion it has served to best me, you are a woman who is firm in her convictions. You are bold, and kind, and you will be an incredible All-Chieftain when the time comes, but you must also remember that to serve your people, you must claim some form of your own happiness. Miserable people make for poor leaders."

Eilis couldn't help but to offer a weak smile in response to his wisdom.

"Eilis, I've seen the two of you together. You are more at ease when he is around you... happier than I've ever seen you, and you... you gentle the rage inside of him. You give him something to live for beyond anger."

"I only hope that's enough now... to give him something to live for."

They sat in silence for several moments, and soon her grandfather rose to leave her in peace. He made his way to the door and had just turned the knob when her voice stopped him.

"Granda?"

"Hm?"

"Would you give your blessing?"

He did not ask her to elaborate, as he instantly understood her meaning, and he took not even a second to consider her request; his response was instant. "Aye. If he lives. You have my word." He gently closed the door behind him.

"He'll live," Eilis whispered to herself. She hoped that if she believed the words enough, that perhaps they would come to fruition.

Eilis smoothed the hair from Albain's brow. The poison was working its way through his system, and the healing herbs were putting up a fair fight. The fever had finally broken, leaving his skin cold and clammy.

She pressed her lips to his forehead. "You'll live," she repeated, hoping that he could somehow hear her.

She pulled another blanket over his massive frame before sliding into the bed next to him. As she so often did, she placed her head upon his chest and listened to his heartbeat, reminding herself that her faithful warrior still fought for his life with all the strength he could manage.

* * *

As he came to, the first thing Albain noticed was the warmth that radiated from his left side; it was the familiar sensation of someone pressed against his body. His eyes fluttered open, and he saw Eilis's sleeping form curled around him. He gave a slight smile to find her in such a state and moved to kiss her cheek, but he was thwarted by a searing pain in his abdomen that shot through his body at the slightest movement. He groaned, which succeeded in jarring her awake.

Upon realizing he had regained consciousness, Eilis gleefully shouted his name. "Albain! Thank the Maker!" She proceeded to cover every inch of his face in a thousand kisses until he could not help but to laugh at the zeal with which she attacked him with affection.

Now that he had returned to her, the strong exterior that Eilis had displayed began to weaken, and Albain saw the tears of relief and gladness, tinged with the vestiges of fear of loss, pool at the corners of her eyes.

"Eilis?"

The sound of her name in his familiar and comforting voice was enough to cause what was left of her composure to falter, and she wept afresh. "I... I was afraid I'd lose you. I couldn't bear it."

Albain's kiss was filled with tenderness, and the salt of her tears was enough to cause his own heart to ache. "You needn't ever fear that. I'll be with you always, if not in body, than in spirit. You are the other half of my soul... by far, the better half."

"You do yourself a disservice to not see you as I do."

Albain chuckled. "Perhaps. But we've a lifetime for you to convince me I'm wrong."

Albain recounted the events that had led him to his

current state. He remembered being accosted by Ser Koth and Ser Romley's cruelty in what he had thought would be his final moments. Further damning was the fact that Eilis's necklace had been recovered from Ser Romley's possession. This, and the documents Eilis had discovered, served King Ruden well in sentencing the two, disgraced knights, along with their conspirator, the traitorous Lord Callor, to death. They were to be held in the castle dungeons until the king and his company departed for Vericus. King Ruden intended to make their executions a very public display, to show that no one—not even his own kin—would be spared from death if they were to betray him.

Albain set to the arduous task of regaining his strength. He practically ate his weight in food and guzzled down pitcher after pitcher of water. It had been several days since he had been attacked, and with the exception of the small quantities of water and broth Eilis had been able to pour down his mouth, his body had been deprived of sustenance.

Gradually, though much too slowly for his liking, Albain's wound began to heal. Heartened by the prospect of a new beginning, and the promise of the All-Chieftain's blessing of their impending union, Albain and Eilis eagerly anticipated their departure from Callor's Rest.

CHAPTER 15

Eilis and Albain descended the winding stairs that led to the dungeons of Callor's Rest. As they drew closer, the air became heavy with cold.

"I can't wait to be rid of this place," muttered Albain.

"Soon, my love. It's only fitting that we bid farewell to our host before we depart."

They reached the entrance to the dungeons where the king's personal guards stood watch. Wordlessly, one of the guards opened the door to allow them to enter.

The dim light of the torches cast long shadows on the floor, and from the darkness peered three faces. Ser Koth's arms, shackled to the wall, hung limply above him. His large legs, too, were chained. Upon seeing Albain, he turned his head away in shame. The Callors had been spared restraints, likely because of their station. The disgraced brothers simultaneously made their way to the front of their cells.

There was unbridled fury and hatred in Ser Romley's eyes, and he immediately set his rage upon Eilis. "You! You cold bitch! After all my brother did for you! This is the way you repay us?"

Eilis silently took a step towards the thick, iron bars that separated her from Ser Romley. Her closed fist flashed forward and connected solidly with Romley's nose. He yelped in pain as blood poured from his nostrils and down the front of his already stained shirt.

Albain chuckled then leaned in close to Romley. "I'd say it wasn't personal, but I won't lie to a dying man. I'm sure your head will make a fine decoration for the walls of Vericus. Such is the fate of traitors."

Selwyn, his face pale and streaked with dirt called out to Eilis. His voice was strained with emotion. "Eilis... I... I'm glad you have come. I didn't think you would. It is truly good to see you. If I'm to die, at least I will have one, last memory of you to call upon in my final moments."

Albain snorted with derision.

"And... I see your Bloodsworn remains by your side," observed Selwyn bitterly.

"Had he died, we wouldn't be having this conversation. The headsman's axe would be a far kinder fate than what I would have done to you."

"I don't doubt your words. Perhaps you'd be doing me a favor. Better death at the hands of one I love than to be paraded through the streets of Vericus as some common criminal and taken as a lamb to slaughter."

"Even now you think your actions righteous. You were never a lamb, Selwyn; you were a wolf in wool. You spoke of progress and returning Allanon to its former glory. Yet, you allied with Evinster and the Talvair."

"Out of necessity. It was a short-term solution that would have paved the path for a glorious future."

"Romley wants to speak of everything you've done for me, Selwyn," remarks Eilis. "Why don't we humor his request? You have given me many things, chief among them death and sorrow. Do you know what the Talvair have done to the Bromus? How they kill our men and rape our women? How even our children are not safe from their barbarism. And you... you gave the Talvair the weapons to kill my people. Let's speak of how your supplies allowed them to continue their assaults against our clans."

"As soon as I came to know you, I ordered the Talvair to cease their attacks."

"Such chivalry! Because you came to love me, you were willing to call off your mercenaries. Truly gallant, Selwyn."

"Yes. I love you, Eilis. Even now. Even after all this! Perhaps... perhaps in another life you will love me back."

"No. After I leave this cell, I will never think of you again," growled Eilis through gritted teeth. "In every life, I will choose Albain."

Involuntarily, Selwyn's hand came to rest on his chest, as if his heart truly were breaking within him. "Everything I have done has been for the betterment of Allanon."

"No. Everything you have done has been for yourself."

"Then you do not understand the meaning of progress. All things seek to improve themselves. To evolve. Sometimes rapid and dramatic change is the only way to achieve that goal. Now Allanon will continue to flounder until it inevitably fails."

"No, Allanon will change for the better when Trystan comes to power... but you and your brother won't be around to see that." Eilis turned towards Ser Koth's cell. "You, on the other hand..."

Ser Koth turned his head to look at her.

"My Bloodsworn personally appealed to the king on your behalf. While you nearly ended his life, we believe you had no part in their larger plot and simply acted on the orders of your lord."

Tears formed in the corners of the giant's eyes, and he nearly wept with gratitude as Eilis summoned one of the guards to open the cell and release him from his chains. As he exited the cell, he paused in front of Albain.

"I..."

Albain raised a hand to silence him. "You needn't explain. I understand duty. But as I've returned your life to you, you owe me something in return."

Ser Koth looked at him questioningly.

"We will have that rematch someday."

A smile tugged at the corners of Ser Koth's lips. "You have my word, Bloodsworn."

❋ ❋ ❋

Eilis and Albain gathered their belongings and met the All-Chieftain in the great hall.

"Are you ready to go home?" he asked his granddaughter.

"I would not be bereft if I never saw Callor's Rest again," returned Eilis.

"You won't have to. I wanted to… I want to apologize for putting you in this mess."

"You couldn't have known."

"I knew you didn't want to come here. That should have been enough."

"You were only trying to help our people."

The All-Chieftain sighed. "I was… However, that should never be at your expense."

"It's all right, Granda. I know that the life of the All-Chieftain is one of sacrifice. You carry the burden of leading and protecting our people. One day, that will be my burden."

The All-Chieftain glanced towards Albain. "At least it is one you can share."

The Bromus loaded their horses and departed Callor's Rest. However, Eilis entreated her grandfather to make a stop on their way out of town.

* * *

The blonde-haired boy sat on the porch and bounced his little sister on his lap while his mother helped their father into the rocking chair nearby. The baby cried miserably; their mother said she was getting new teeth, and the pain was making her fussy.

"Now, now, Lydi," soothed Lark. "How about a song then?"

"All the heather in the valley will bow down and swoon
At the very first light of the great silver moon
The stars, they are shining
And though it is dark
They will vanish at once when the old meadowlark
Sings a song in an attempt to bid you awake
And when you open your eyes
My hand you will take

We will walk by the river and out to the sea
And I swear to you, darling, one day you'll see
The Maker will cherish and bless you small child
For the love that I give you
Can't be measured in miles."

Lydi giggled and clutched her brother's cheeks with her grimy hands.

"You're such a good big brother, Lark," remarked his mother with a smile.

The sounds of hoofbeats emanated from down the road, and a cloud of dust heralded the approach of several riders.

Sebastian reached for his crutch and struggled to his feet; his devoted wife helped to support him.

"There you are, love," she said.

"Thank you, Alice," he replied gratefully. His lips brushed against her cheek.

Lark held his hand over his forehead to block the brightness of the early morning sun. "Mum! Da! It's Eilis and Albain!"

The company stopped their horses near the farmhouse.

"Eilis!" cried Lark. He carried Lydi with him as he greeted his friend.

Eilis dismounted and approached the boy. "Good morning, Lark. And hello, Lydi." She reached out and held the girl's tiny fingers in her hand.

"Good morning!" called Sebastian. "If all we've heard in the town is true, we thought you had put Callor's Rest far behind you by now."

"We're on our way back to our homelands, but we wanted to stop and say goodbye first," explained Eilis. "And Lark, I wanted to introduce you to someone."

The All-Chieftain came to stand by his granddaughter's side.

"This is my Granda."

Both Lark and his father gaped in disbelief to be in such

113

close proximity to the legendary Seamus Oakheart.

"You're really him!" cried Lark. "Seamus the Strong! We saw you at the tournament, but you're really here!" Lark poked him in the stomach as if to make sure his senses weren't eluding him.

The All-Chieftain chuckled in amusement. "Aye, I am. Eilis has told me all about you."

"She has? All... of it?"

The All-Chieftain winked. "All of it."

Lark reddened in embarrassment.

"You're a good lad for trying to help your family. Nothing in the world is more important than kin." He squeezed Eilis's shoulder. "I've a gift for you." Seamus said to the boy. He reached into his leather sporran and extracted a round, flat piece of silver, about the size of a coin. It had been stamped with the symbol of the Oakhearts. "You keep this safe, eh? If you or your family are ever in need of help—no matter what it is—you show this to any Bromus, and they'll know you're kin to the Oak Clan. They'll get word to me." He placed the token in the boy's trembling hand.

Lark's lip quivered with emotion. He wrapped his thin arms around the All-Chieftain's waist in an embrace. Seamus hoisted him into the air and spun him around as if he weighed nothing. The boy cackled with glee, and when he was good and dizzy, Seamus plunked him down on the ground.

"Now, we best be on our way. You be sure to heed your Mum and Da, and be good to your sister. You hear?"

Lark nodded, his expression serious. "I will. Promise I will."

"Aye. Good lad."

Eilis bid the family farewell and gave Lark a long embrace before she and her grandfather mounted their horses again.

Albain directed his mount towards the farmhouse and came to a stop in front of Lark. Wordlessly, he reached his hand into his saddlebag and extracted a large pouch filled with gold—his winnings from the tournament—and tossed it into the boy's hands.

He turned his horse in Eilis's direction as calls of "Thank you, Albie! Goodbye!" rang out behind him.

Eilis moved her horse closer to her Bloodsworn's steed and took a deep breath as the gentle rays of the sun washed over her. "We're going home, Albain."

"Home," he repeated.

EPILOGUE

After the executions of Lord Callor and Ser Romley, King Ruden honored the Bromus by officially recognizing their sovereignty as an independent nation and pledging the aid of Allanon in their continued fight against the Talvair. The Bromus, bolstered by the king's soldiers, managed to decimate the Talvair and sent their remaining forces fleeing back into Evinster.

Eilis and Albain returned home to the lands of the Oak Clan where they fulfilled their promise to each other to be wed.

* * *

The silken folds of her white dress fell around her; she looked akin to a whimsical faerie queen from the olden tales of Allanon. Her brown eyes sparkled with emotion, and she bit her lip anxiously as she held her hands out to her sides.

"Well? Will he like it?" she asked hopefully.

The bodice of her dress was adorned with a silver oak tree, and the silken train that was spread out behind her had a stripe of dark blue velvet emblazoned with another silver oak tree.

"Don't be afraid if he says nothing. He'll be as speechless as I am right now," replied Prince Trystan with a laugh. "You look radiant, Eilis." He took her by the hands and placed a chaste kiss on her cheek. The prince glanced down at the ground and took note of the visible signs of wear in the grass. "I had thought Rose had been kidding about you pacing a hole in the ground. Second thoughts?"

"No," she answered firmly. "Never. I just... I want this to be perfect for him. Have you seen my groom today?"

Trystan nodded. "Clobbering poor fools in the sparring ring. I think he's as anxious as you are, but for all the right reasons. He's marrying the woman of his dreams. What man wouldn't be overwhelmed at the thought of that?"

Eilis smiled and cast a knowing glance between Trystan and Rose. "Maybe one day I'll get to have this same talk with you, Trystan."

Rose blushed and nearly dropped the bouquets of flowers she had been tasked with carrying. She quickly shoved one into Eilis's hands and turned abruptly towards the front door of Eilis and Albain's marital home. "Shall we then? Hate to keep the crowd waiting."

Trystan offered Eilis his arm, and she looped her own through his. They made their way outside and watched as Rose descended the hill ahead of them. The former thief was unaccustomed to walking in such ornate shoes and nearly tumbled when she drew close to the arbor.

Albain's entire body was consumed by nervous energy. He eagerly wished to look upon his bride, but it was Bromus custom that the groom did not lay eyes on the bride until she reached his side at the altar.

The gathered crowd stood as the heirs to the King and All-Chieftain drew closer.

There was a sharp intake of breath from the Old Oakheart as he witnessed his granddaughter's approach. "She's... she's beautiful."

"She's always beautiful," came Albain's quiet reply.

Unabashed tears streamed down the All-Chieftain's face as his granddaughter drew nearer. He took a moment to collect himself then cleared his throat.

"Prince Trystan Elidure, in so presenting the bride this day, will you join her hand with that of her beloved?" directed the All-Chieftain.

Trystan placed Eilis's hand in Albain's outstretched one. Albain's long hair had been brushed back neatly and tied with a red ribbon. His beard had been neatly trimmed and there was a faint smell of soap emanating from his freshly washed skin. The towering warrior was dressed in a black, silk shirt and his finest black and red Cur Clan tartan great kilt.

He turned to look at Eilis.

His knees nearly buckled beneath him, and his heart pounded so loudly that he thought it might erupt from within. His lip quivered slightly, and tears of gladness pooled at the corners of his eyes.

He was undone.

Albain drew in a ragged breath as he pressed Eilis's hands to his lips.

"Donalbain Roric McCann," began the All-Chieftain.

Rose emitted a sharp bark of laughter at this revelation of Albain's full name. "*Donalbain?*"

Albain turned and gave her a sharp look, but there was the slightest twist in the corners of his lips as he returned his attention to the All-Chieftain.

"And Eilis Andelynn Oakheart," continued the All-Chieftain. "The Marriage Vow is a sacred vow. It is unbreakable, and once spoken cannot be recanted. We believe in life after death, and that the death of the body does not sever the marriage pact. If it is indeed your intention to bind yourselves together by heart and by soul for all of eternity, then you may speak your vows to one another."

Albain and Eilis turned to face each other, and she took his hands in her own.

As she began to speak, her voice quavered with emotion. "I didn't know what love was or could be until I met you. You're my first thought when I wake, and my last thought when I sleep. You have done more for me than I can possibly express. For every fault I own, you are my perfect balance. I will love you with all my heart and soul. I will be yours and yours alone. I will honor you and cherish you for all our days, and all that comes after." Eilis fought back the tears that welled in her eyes, and the smile she cast up at her beloved was dazzling in its purity. She reached up her hands and pressed them against his cheeks, one smooth and the other grievously scarred. "Before the Maker, will you receive my vows, Albain?"

"I will."

From a leather sheath hanging at her side, Eilis produced a small but ornate dagger. A light blue gem adorned the top of the handle. She placed the tip of the dagger against her palm and dragged it against her skin, producing a line of crimson blood.

"You are blood of my blood," she spoke to Albain. "You are bone of my bone. I give you my body that we two might be one. I give you my spirit. My heart is your home. In life and in death, you are never alone."

A look of pride and pure love softened Albain's features, and for a moment, it was as if he forgot the crowd of well-wishers that looked on. His focus was solely on the woman before him. Every Talvair who ever lived could storm through the ceremony or the sun could fall from the sky, and still Albain could not force himself to look away from her for an instant.

His gravelly voice, often so sharp, was gentle as he addressed Eilis. "I should have died a thousand times over, and I never could figure out why the Maker chose to let me linger on this earth. I know now. It was so I could meet you. You make me want to be better. Eilis, will you take my vow?"

Eilis smiled. "I will."

He took the dagger from Eilis's hand and drew the blade against his own palm.

"Eilis, you are blood of my blood. You are bone of my bone. I give you my body that we two might be one. I give you my spirit. My heart is your home. In life and in death, you are never alone."

Eilis and Albain pressed their bloodied palms together.

"Bound by blood, heart, and soul," spoke the All-Chieftain. "Let no man, nor life, nor death dissever the vows you have spoken this day."

The All-Chieftain gave a slight nod of his head, and Albain and Eilis joined in a passionate kiss, much to the whoops and delight of the assembled masses.

"It is time for you to claim your clan," announced the All-Chieftain.

Albain, still holding the dagger, extended the handle towards Eilis who looked back at him with conviction in her eyes.

Eilis stepped back from the arbor, and without the slightest hesitation, she passed by the Oak Clan banner and stood under the Cur Clan banner.

A hush fell over the crowd as Eilis reached up and cut the banner from its fastenings on the post. Her expression serious and not the slightest bit reluctant, she carried the banner to her grandfather who held it aloft for all to see.

"The McCanns claim the Cur Clan."

Despite the genuine shock and murmurs of surprise that rippled through the crowd, the All-Chieftain smiled slightly, as if he had expected this turn of events. After all, she was his granddaughter, and Eilis shared the stubbornness of her kin.

Albain stared at Eilis in wonder. "Are... are you certain?"

She nodded before turning to the crowd. "The Cur Clan has long been on the verge of extinction, but what once was one is now two, and we welcome any and all who wish to join us. The legacy of *our* clan has been a dark one, but I vow to bring honor to its name. As heir to the All-Chieftain, it is my wish that my husband be recognized as Chieftain of the Cur Clan," spoke Eilis.

Albain's eyes widened in shock and for a moment he looked like a deer that had been cornered by a hunter.

"He has proven himself in service to our people time and time again, and as the only natural surviving member of the Cur Clan, I believe it is his right," she continued.

The All-Chieftain considered this for a moment then nodded his head in agreement. "It will be done."

"We also request our rightful place on the Council."

Again, the All-Chieftain nodded in consent.

Albain had spent much of his life alone, as an outcast among his people, and he was certain that the Cur Clan would die with him. To know that his wife had chosen to revive his clan rather than pledge their newly formed family to her birth clan touched Albain's heart in a way he hadn't thought possible.

As Albain and Eilis stood before all who had assembled to witness their vows, the warrior couldn't help but to wonder why the Maker had blessed him so completely. For once, hope had prevailed, and despite all odds, he was now husband to the woman he loved.

After the ceremony and subsequent feast to celebrate their nuptials had concluded, Albain swept his bride into his arms and carried her to the newly constructed house that would become their home. It was perfect in its simplicity, and they were eager to begin their lives together in a place they would fill will love, laughter, and someday—if the Maker willed it—little ones.

Albain gently set Eilis down before him, and she stood on her tiptoes to beseech a kiss from him. Her lips were soft and her mouth moved tenderly against his own.

His hands rested on the small of her back, and she wrapped her arms around his waist as he deepened the kiss. Her lips moved to the side of his neck, and the gentle suck followed by a soft bite resulted in a sharp intake of breath from the Bloodsworn.

He was overcome with a desperate need to relieve her of that beautiful dress. His fingers fumbled with the laces at the back of the bodice, and her laughter at his expense made his heart swell.

"These strings are the devil!" he muttered into her ear. Finally, he managed to loosen them, and she slid the gown to the floor.

Albain drank in her beauty. Her dark, brown hair cascaded over her bare shoulders, and her eyes sparkled with an intensity that loudly proclaimed her want for him.

"You are..." His words stuck in his throat. How could he possibly bring voice to the depth of his feelings for her? How could he adequately express the awe that overwhelmed him as he gazed upon her?

Luckily, he did not have to struggle any further to form words, as again her lips crashed into his own.

She relieved him of his shirt, and his kilt quickly joined the growing pile of clothing on the freshly sanded floor of their new house, a place that already felt like home.

He gasped as she took him in her hand, her soft palm applying light strokes that increased in pressure and speed.

He cupped her breasts and massaged them gently, causing her to let out a sigh of pleasure. He bent his mouth to suck, his tongue playing across her nipple and making her cheeks flush.

"Albain... I *want* you."

He froze.

He had lived a life where people tolerated his presence and looked upon him with suspicion, and sometimes even hatred.

Now, this incomparable woman—his *wife*—*wanted* him, and only him, for the rest of their days.

"Then you shall have me." His voice was strained with emotion he hadn't expected.

Again, he swept her into his arms, carried her to their bedroom, and placed her upon their marital bed. He reclined beside her, and allowed his mouth and hands to explore her body and coax sounds of pleasure from her. He hadn't thought it was possible, but those soft murmurs and affirmations of love, his name upon her lips coming in whispers then shouts, nearly caused him to lose his composure before he had a chance to be within her.

She parted her legs, inviting him to enter, his length and girth filling her place completely and eliciting a moan of pleasure as he thrust within her. He delved deeper, her warmth invigorating his entire form. Her hands roved over his back, on his shoulders, and down his arms as they continued their lovemaking.

"Albain... I love you."

It was her words that tipped him over the thin precipice he had been clinging to. His body shuddered as she tightened around him, and they rode the wave of their climax together.

They wasted no time in their pursuit of the goal of expanding their family, and by the time the moon shone through their bedroom window, their marriage had been consummated more than once.

* * *

Weeks turned into months, and Albain's awe over his good fortune did not diminish. Albain awoke every morning to find Eilis firmly wrapped in his arms. So many nights he had yearned for her company, and now he would be blessed by waking next to her every day for the rest of his life.

They had settled into their own version of domestic bliss. The once Clanless Albain became a well-respected member of the Bromus community, and Eilis continued to serve as an inspiration and pillar of strength for her people.

One evening, Albain returned from training some of the young Bromus warriors who continually sought him out for his wisdom in combat.

"Are you hungry? There's plenty of supper left. I kept it warm for you over the fire," informed Eilis.

"Aye. It smelled so delicious I could feel it beckoning me from halfway across the camp. And I am hungry... but not for that." He gave her a suggestive look before glancing towards their bed.

"I see," she laughed.

He buried his face against her neck and kissed her over and over, his beard tickling her and causing her to cry out in glee. Without further delay, he carried her to their bed.

He took his time, exploring every inch of her body and calling upon all of his knowledge of their previous encounters to provide the greatest depth of pleasure that he could bestow upon her.

Every aspect of her drove him absolutely wild: the way the soft lines of her body were illuminated by the light from the fire, the way her dark hair fell across her bare shoulders, the way she gazed upon him with unbridled adoration, and the soft sound of contentment she gave when she had claimed her pleasure.

Afterwards, they remained firmly entwined with each other, neither willing to break their embrace and brave the cold outside of the blankets and furs that cocooned them.

Eventually, Eilis gazed up at him sleepily, love and affection reflected in her bleary-eyed gaze. When she nodded off, he held her tightly against him. Despite his grumbling stomach and the continuing wafting smells of delicious food still warming on the fire, he couldn't bring himself to leave her company for even a moment, and instead lovingly admired the sweet simplicity of his wife resting in his arms.

When he awoke the following morning, he found himself spellbound by the peaceful expression of contentment on his lover's face. The rays of light that shone through the windows of their simple abode fell upon her sleeping form. He swept his hand through her dark hair, which fell across her tanned shoulders in delicate waves. Soon, she began to stir, and he greeted her with a lingering kiss. They lay together in a state of serenity until she finally broke the silence.

"It's almost sunrise, and I could do with some fresh air. Will you walk with me, my love?"

They dressed and departed from their home. Albain offered Eilis his arm, and they quietly strolled along the side of the winding creek that cut through much of the Bromus lands.

"There are none left," he said quietly.

"None left? What do you mean?" she inquired.

"I have given you my life in two ways, by the only two vows our people hold dear: first, as your Bloodsworn, and now, as your husband. I'd give you the world if I could, but somehow even that is less than you deserve. You are far more than I could have ever hoped for. What more can I offer you now that I have nothing left to give?"

A soft smile graced her features, and as she so often did, she caressed the scarred side of his face.

"This."

Leaning against him, she stood upon her tiptoes, and he

gladly indulged her by tilting his head down to her until their noses touched.

His lips claimed hers, and he was filled with the same overwhelming sense of love that affected him every time he thought of her or was blessed by her presence.

Before, their kisses had always been rushed in stolen moments, but now they were able to take their time, luxuriating in such simple but meaningful proclamations of love, and he was in no hurry for it to end.

He rested a hand on her hip and was reluctant to let her go for even a moment for fear that he would wake to find all this had been part of some miraculous dream, but the soft smile upon her face, the sweet scent of her skin, the deep brown of her eyes, and the exhilarating feel of her hands in his could not be faked. This was real; she was his wife, and this was now his future.

He ran his fingers through her hair, twirling it lightly on his fingertips. "To think... The Cur Clan was all but extinct; now its strength has doubled."

Eilis was thoughtful for a moment. "You are partly right." Eilis took her husband's hand and gently placed it over her abdomen.

Albain looked at her quizzically, and it took several moments for him to grasp her meaning, but when he finally did, he swept her into a long embrace, holding her tightly against him. When he reluctantly released her from his grasp, she saw tears of gladness forming in his eyes.

He knelt before her and pressed a kiss upon the place where their child grew. He thought of how his own father had failed him, and how he desperately wished to be a far better man, and an infinitely better father.

"Then there's one more vow I need to make."

ACKNOWLEDGEMENTS

Bloodsworn: Three Vows could not have been completed without the support of many people.

Thank you to my beta readers: Kim, Julie, Rachel, and Sara for taking the time to look over early drafts of this piece and providing me with your feedback.

Chris Shearer of Swatara Media continues to lend his artistic genius and tireless efforts to translating my muddled visions into beautiful cover art.

Sara—my friend, editor, co-conspirator, and co-founder of Writers 4 a Purpose—you have often commiserated with me and served as a sounding board for my ideas and writing-induced tantrums. I cannot thank you enough for loving *The Stolen Heir Series* and its characters as much as I do. Thank you for talking me out of my own head when I considered abandoning this piece.

Matt, your incredible dedication to our family, your tireless support of my work, and your unconditional love are a blessing to me every day. You are the greatest husband in the world, and I could not have done this without you. *"You are blood of my blood. You are bone of my bone. I give you my body that we two might be one. I give you my spirit. My heart is your home. In life and in death, you are never alone."*

Ben and Ash you are—and will always be—the loves of my life. I am so incredibly proud of both of you, and I am beyond lucky to be your mom. (P.S. You better not be reading this book if you're under 18, because the idea of you reading the romance scenes totally weirds me out.)

Last, but not least, thank you to all of the readers who have followed me into the land of Allanon and helped to bring these characters to life.

ABOUT THE AUTHOR

Val Cates

Val Cates is a teacher, author, and one of the founders of Writers 4 A Purpose. Bloodsworn: Three Vows is an alternative timeline tale that features characters from her debut novel, A Gift of Name.

Val is an equal opportunity writer. She does not confine herself to a specific genre, format, or audience. She appreciates all of these things for the uniqueness they offer.

When Val is not writing, she spends most of her days educating the next generation of writers in her English-Language Arts classroom. She also hosts a series of videos on social media geared towards educating and inspiring fellow writers. Val enjoys spending time with her family, eating copious amounts of chocolate, awaiting her overdue letter from Hogwarts, and wondering if her teaching superpowers could be useful in the Marvel Universe.

Val lives in Pennsylvania, where winter is too cold, summer is too humid, but fall is heaven on earth. For more information and to follow Val's work, visit

www.valcates.com